May 13, 1776

I feel as if the whole of Dunmore's fleet is holding its breath, waiting. Galen and I have been on board for not three full weeks, yet we are anxious and growing well weary of life on the Emma with no sign of battle. The only sights we see are the other ships, the far shores of the Elizabeth River, and each other. As much as Galen and Ammiel and Joseph are my friends, I do tire of their constant visage.

I have yet to see Lord Dunmore, the man for whom we have come to fight. I can see the flag on his ship when I am on the main deck, but that flag is silent. What are his thoughts? What are his plans?

This morning another of the Ethiopian Regiment, a fellow named Percy, perished of the smallpox. With God's grace neither Ammiel, Galen, nor I have succumbed to this wicked disease. The steward's mate has, however, and has taken to his hammock. He was replaced with a mute boy, a sailor, who does his job without complaint.

But if we could only fight! Bring me a slave owner and a pistol and let us have our destinies!

Tor Books by Elizabeth Massie

*forthcoming

YOUNG FOUNDERS

1776:

SON OF LIBERTY

A Novel of the American Revolution

Elizabeth Massie

TOR®

A TOM DOHERTY ASSOCIATES BOOK
NEW YORK

This is a work of fiction. All the characters and events portrayed in this book are either products of the author's imagination or are used fictitiously.

1776: SON OF LIBERTY

A Tor Book
Published by Tom Doherty Associates, LLC
175 Fifth Avenue
New York, NY 10010

www.tor.com

Tor® is a registered trademark of Tom Doherty Associates, LLC.

ISBN: 0-812-59094-5

First edition: July 2000

Printed in the United States of America

0   9   8   7   6   5   4   3   2   1

❧ Introduction ❧

We hold these Truths to be self-evident,
that all men are created equal. . . .

BOLD AND INSPIRING words.
But little wonder the 500,000 African-
American slaves in the colonies who embraced this
"self-evident" truth as enshrined in the Declaration
of Independence bitterly resented the fact that
they were exempted from its sweeping claim of independence and individual sovereignty.

Were not African Americans "Men" in the eyes
of colonial America? The answer: most emphati-
cally, no.

When hostilities between England and the colonies erupted in 1775 no more than 25,000 African Americans out of 500,000 were "free blacks."
The overwhelming percentage of slaves was con-
centrated on plantations in the rural South. But
slavery at least before 1777 was not an exclusively
Southern problem. If the slave population of the
North was smaller it might have had less to do with
enlightened attitudes toward race and more that
the expanding cities of the urbanized North were
less dependent on cheap and plentiful labor than

the agrarian South. For instance, in 1712 a group of black slaves was publicly executed by officials in New York for inspiring a plot to win their freedom through force. Nevertheless, between 1777 and 1804 all states north of Maryland outlawed slavery.

Briefly, the cause of the American Revolution was this: American colonists, thousands of miles removed from the authority of the British parliament, increasingly came to resent any sign of interference by the Crown in colonial affairs. The British, on the other hand, saddled with enormous debt after their exhausting war against France over control of North America, looked to the increasingly prosperous colonies for relief. Compromise evaporated as each side chose to harden its position. The British were outraged to be dictated to by uppity and ungrateful colonial upstarts. The Americans chanted independence and invoked the ideals of liberty and freedom from heartless tyranny.

War became inevitable.

When antagonisms between the British and the Americans reached a crescendo, blacks—both free and slave—answered the call. A runaway slave named Crispus Attucks was the first man killed in the fight for independence when British soldiers shot him and four others dead in the infamous Boston Massacre in 1770. At least five blacks were recorded as having served honorably at Lexington.

The British actively recruited blacks to the British cause. In exchange for military service slaves were promised freedom and often stakes of land after the war. In 1775 Lord Dunmore, the colonial governor of Virginia, issued a blanket proclamation of emancipation to all blacks who fought against the rebels. Tens of thousands of blacks es-

caped plantations and more than one thousand—
often in guerilla gangs called banditti—looted and
pillaged plantations and helped other slaves escape to freedom.

Dunmore's promise proved hollow, however, as
many blacks who served the British would tragi-
cally discover. As the years went by and the British
cause became hopeless, Dunmore had many of the
black soldiers in the Crown's ranks captured and
sold back into slavery.

A dire shortage of colonial recruits forced General George Washington to reconsider his ban on
African-American soldiers. In 1778 Congress at last
approved a resolution calling for the enlistment of
blacks in the American army. By the war's end
more than 5,000 slaves from all the states except
Georgia and South Carolina had served honorably
and with commendable distinction. Plantation masters could avoid military service by having slaves
serve in their place. Many slaves did and thereby
won their freedom.

Discrimination against blacks was widespread,
and many regiments were segregated. But most
were integrated. Ironically, it would be more than
170 years—at the outbreak of the Korean War—
before blacks would again serve in integrated military units.

The American Revolution brought independence to white colonial America. But for African
Americans the road to freedom that they had
spilled blood to build hit an unwelcoming brick
wall. According to the first census of 1790 the population of free blacks had risen from 25,000 to
60,000. But the slave population had climbed to
nearly 700,000.

What did it mean to be a "free black"?

Not much. Four states, Indiana, Wisconsin, Michigan, and Iowa, prohibited blacks from immigrating. Blacks attempting to relocate to Illinois were threatened with bondage. A series of "black codes" passed in Ohio established codes of behavior that blacks were forced to adhere to before they could take up residence.

Overall, free blacks faced hostility and discrimination in almost every aspect of life. Most blacks were barred from enrolling in schools, and complex restrictions limited the kinds of businesses in which they were allowed to be employed. Voting was out of the question. Blacks were even restricted in what and where they could worship.

The American Revolution ended what many thought was an unjust system and replaced it with a government dedicated to free expression and independence and committed to the ideals of freedom and liberty.

It would be another hundred years until the United States would find itself torn apart by a bloody civil war whose outcome would determine what freedom ultimately meant. Even then the outcome was in doubt. It would not be until 1964—a full hundred years after the end of the Civil War—that landmark civil rights legislation would put into law ideals enshrined in the rhetoric of freedom.

We hold these Truths to be self-evident, that all Men are created equal. . . .

The struggle for freedom and equality continues.

1

March 4, 1766
Cleb.
Caleb.
My nam is Caleb.
My name is Caleb.
I am six yers old.
I am lerning to rite.
I am learning to wite.
I go to scool.
I go to schol.
School. School.
Caleb.
Caleb.

2

May 30, 1766
My name is Caleb Jacobson.
Mrs Donahby teaches me.
With the quaker boys.
Jesus Chist.
Jesus Christ.
God the Fathre.
Holy Ghost.
My name is Caleb.
In Adam's fall we sinned all.
Our Fathir Who Art in Heven, hallow'd be Thy Name.
Pece be with us.
Forever and ever ammen.
My name is Caleb.

3

THE ROLLING ROAD passed Adam Donaughby's farm, traveling along the southern border of the property like the soiled and ragged hem of a woman's gown, a broad path of hard-packed earth with sprigs of determined chicory cutting through here and there. The road was most traveled in the summer and fall, when the wilderness farms of western Maryland had their loads of tobacco ready to take to the warehouses on the river near Baltimore. Hogsheads packed with dried tobacco would rumble down the road, powered by horse, oxen, or black men. The remaining traffic consisted of salesmen's wagons, couriers, and occasional folk on their way to visit family in the far reaches of the colony.

Six-year-old Caleb Jacobson stood by the rail fence of Adam Donaughby's property, clutching a sack of thorny raspberry bushes and a small shovel, and staring at the fight going on in the middle of the road. It was a mighty battle on a small scale. Two chipmunks had found each other, and had flung themselves on each other with a vengeance, with flying fur and chattering teeth. Little feet kicked, little noses flared. Every few seconds one would hop high in the air and come down again, as if trying to show his opponent he was bigger than he actually was.

"Ho there!" Caleb called to the chipmunks. "Stop that!"

The chipmunks rolled in the dust. One freed himself from the tangle, ran several feet away, then turned back to bare his teeth.

"Stop that!" shouted Caleb.

The little creatures dove at each other. Caleb scooped up several pieces of rock from beneath the tangle of fragrant honeysuckle along the fence bottom and hurled them at the chipmunks. They landed with a click and a clatter. The startled animals fell away from each other and ran into the weeds beside the road.

"You aren't supposed to fight!" Caleb said to the spot in the weeds where the chipmunks had disappeared. "Fighting is the devil's work!"

A crow overhead cawed as if in answer, then settled on the top branch of a roadside cedar tree.

The day was early, but though cloudy, it was quite hot and humid already. It was July 4 of 1766, and there had been no rain in nearly three weeks. Caleb wore only a pair of breeches with the hems unbuttoned at his knee. He wore no shirt as it was too hot. He wore no shoes because he had no shoes. But his feet were used to the rocks and rough ground of the Donaughby farm. He was born there, and had lived his life there. He knew where the worst of the thistle patches liked to grow and where skin-biting outcroppings of stone hid among the weeds.

He shifted the sack of raspberry bushes from one shoulder to the other, and looked at the crow on the treetop. The bird sat as if it was a king, its sleek black feathers glistening in the sunlight.

"What's on your mind, bird?" asked Caleb. "What'dya see from way up there? A town? The ocean? Is it a pretty thing, with ships and sails? Mama says it's so."

The bird blinked and tipped his head silently. What secrets it could see, it would not share.

As Caleb turned from the fence, the sound of hoof beats on the road pulled him back around. The boy had never been off the Quaker's farm; he and his mother had their duties and their place in a hut on the bottom land of the Donaughby farm. But Caleb always stopped to see who was coming and going on the rolling road. He always wondered who they were, what they were up to, and where they were headed.

Today it was a lone rider, leaning over the pommel of his saddle and staring ahead as if in a daydream, leading another man at the end of a long rope. The man on the horse was dressed in breeches, tall boots, and a waistcoat, and his eyes were shaded beneath a tri-cornered black hat.

The man behind the horse wore a thin pair of pants, a dirty shirt, and a floppy hat pulled down over his eyes far enough that Caleb couldn't see his face. There were dust-coated rags tied around his feet. The man's hands were bound with the rope that the rider held. The man on the horse was white. The man on the ground was black. Like Caleb.

Caleb watched as the horse clopped along, heading east, and the black man stumbled behind. Every few seconds his rope-bound hands would jerk upward because he was not keeping pace with the horse. Shadows from the roadside trees strummed the travelers like fingers on a silent banjo.

"Hello there!" called Caleb. "Where you going?"

The rider did not respond. He just swiped mucus from his nose with his fist. The man on the ground glanced up. His eyes were dark, his face streaked with dirt. He gave Caleb a slow nod that seemed to be either a greeting or a warning.

"Caleb!" came a distant voice from over the knoll behind him. "Where are you? Get home now!"

Caleb scrambled up the sloping land. As he dug his toes into the dry grass, his thoughts lingered on the black man back on the road. He had asked his mother before about men he'd seen walking east and west on the rolling road, but she said very little other than, "Slavery's the devil's doin', son. I lived it." Then she would get quiet and Caleb would ask no more. *Slavery*. A strange word that meant men and women with damaged feet and heavy loads, people with bent heads or blazing eyes.

Caleb reached the top of the hill and paused to catch his breath. From this vantage point he could see most of Adam Donaughby's 100-acre farm, "Quality and Quantity." Straight ahead across the cattle field was the Quaker family's log farmhouse, the outhouse, smokehouse, hooded well, and shed in which Mrs. Donaughby held school for the Quaker boys in the spring and fall. To the right of the house was a garden in which Mrs. Donaughby raised staples for her growing family of daughters—beans, turnips, cabbage. Corn stalks

waved in the hot breeze, shimmering like green
water over stones in the creek.

Behind the farmhouse was the stable and the
wide pasture reserved for the horses. A stream cut
through the farmland, following an irregular path
from north woods to southeast woods, from horse
pasture to cattle field, its banks lined with reeds,
rattley briars, and stalks of milkweed with near-
bursting pods. To the far left of the cattle field,
down on the low land near the creek, was a small
building which had once been a hay barn. Now,
flanked by its own sheds, gardens, and rough fencing, it was the home of Caleb Jacobson and his
mother, Francis.

Francis Jacobson was outside the door of the
hut, her hands on her hips. Her hair was covered
with a white bonnet and her plain black skirt bil-
lowed in the breeze. Caleb could tell by the way
she was standing that she was frowning. Caleb had
been sent out to collect raspberry bushes but he'd
become distracted with animals he'd found—a
snake shedding its skin, and then the chipmunks—
and now he was late.

Caleb's mother worked for Mrs. Donaughby
every afternoon and evening, helping the Quaker
woman with her daughters and her cooking. Francis had adopted the Quaker dress and beliefs soon
after Caleb's birth. There were certain behaviors
expected by God, the Quakers believed. One such
behavior was punctuality. It was disrespectful to
make someone wait, for it was acting as a thief of
time.

Caleb clutched the shovel and sack and ran
down the hill. He did not run like children would
normally run, but with a heavy beat to his right
foot and a skip to his left, galloping as he had seen

Mr. Donaughby's horses gallop on a windy afternoon. He imagined he was riding one of the magnificent beasts, and could feel the thunderous hoofs beneath him, rhythmic and pounding. Ba-BOOM! Ba-BOOM! He dodged lazy cattle swishing flies with their tails and piles of steaming manure. He jumped the stream with ease, landing with a grunt on the other side and not losing his stride or the sack-load of bushes. A cluster of yellow butterflies scattered from his path like bits of sunlight caught in a whirlwind.

"Caleb!" called his mother. "Have you feet of molasses?"

Caleb reached the narrow path that connected the Jacobson hut with the Donaughby farmhouse on the other side of the cattle field, and followed it to the fence, through the gate, and to the doorstep. He dropped the sack and the shovel, said "Got four!," then gave his mother a big grin.

But it didn't change the inevitable.

Francis gave Caleb six healthy swats on the backside. Caleb grit his teeth and waited for it to be over. It was never enough to really hurt; Francis didn't believe in raising a hand to cause pain to another, but she did believe in making her anger clear.

"Boy!" She spun him around and put her face close to his. Her one good eye was bright with intent; her other eye, burned to uselessness before Caleb was born, stared at him like the eye of God, unblinking, unknowable, seeing nothing of the world but certainly the depths of Caleb's soul.

"I'm late to Mrs. Donaughby's 'cause of you!" Francis said. Her breath smelled of cabbage and souring milk. "She's baking today, and here I am, worried sick about you! You are not to leave the yard while I am gone! Understand me?"

Caleb nodded.

"Do your chores then practice your letters."

"Yes'am," said Caleb.

Francis shook her head and her finger. The dead eye held its mysterious gaze. "Should make you go with me to tell Mrs. Donaughby you're sorry. You know I couldn't leave this house 'til I knew you were safe. What if a bear had got you? Or a wolf? Or worse, a—" She stopped herself, and shook her head. "There's lots of things to snatch up a boy, to take you away to hard places afar," she said quietly. "But you're safe, thank the Lord." She gave Caleb one last swat, this one more of a pat, and trudged off up the path that led to the Donaughby house.

Caleb watched his mother go, her shoulders driven forward, her skirt flapping. Francis Jacobson was not an old woman, at least not as old as Mrs. Donaughby and the Quaker ladies who came to visit the farm on occasion. Francis was twenty-three. But her face was thin and bony, and life hung on her like a heavy blanket.

Caleb knew that his mother had been a slave back in New York. He knew she had had a husband named George, who was Caleb's father, and who was drowned in the East River while trying to save another man's life. Francis had worked for a family named the Lewises, and had been given her free papers after a fire in the kitchen had gotten out of control and had burned Francis nearly to death and surely to no good as a house servant, for the Lewises were of a wealthy family who took their station seriously, and a maimed slave was an embarrassment. After her recovery, Francis had walked to Maryland in search of her sister, Onnie, whom she hadn't seen in four years. Francis had not found Onnie, however. Four days into Maryland, some miles east of here, she had been attacked by a wolf. Mr. Donaughby had come upon her with his rifle, and had killed the wolf. He took her to his farm, where Mrs. Donaughby nursed her back to health. The family then provided the hay barn as a home for Francis and the baby who was soon to be delivered.

Caleb left the heat of the outdoors for the inside of the hut, stepping over the threshold into the pleasant coolness. In the fireplace, coals danced with an orange glow. One of Caleb's chores was to keep the fire burning low all day so that meals could be cooked and clothes could be washed and embers could be taken outside to stoke for a candle-dipping fire or soap-boiling fire.

On the hearth by the fire was a large pot in which was some potato and pork stew, left over from breakfast and intended for dinner and supper. Caleb scooped out a glob of still-warm stew with his hand, and sucked his fingers until the food and the flavor was gone. Caleb then studied his fingers. Those on his left hand were normal, but the last three fingers on his right hand were fused together to the last knuckle. He'd been born this way, but having three attached fingers had never been a problem except that Jeremiah Martin, who went to Mrs. Donaughby's school along with Caleb and the other boys, made sport of it. When Mrs. Donaughby could not hear, Jeremiah would sing, "Paddle paw, paddle paw, Your mother broke the Lord's good law!"

Caleb knew his mother had done nothing wrong for him to have a hand such as he did. Francis had explained his deformity to him. When she had been with child, a hawk had swooped down upon her in the field, startling her so badly that she had swooned, and lay unconscious until a grazing cow awakened her. Two months later, Caleb was born with a hand shaped more like a wing than a hand. But it was nothing of which to be ashamed, Francis explained. She had done nothing wrong, nor had he.

Caleb got up from the stool, put the lid back on the pot, and got the broom from the corner by the door. The first chore was to chase outside all the summer grit that had found its way inside since yesterday.

The Jacobson hut was a cozy, one-room structure. Though once the hay barn, it had been altered with a bark-shingled roof, a door that latched, two shuttered windows, a rough wooden floor, and the simple stone fireplace. Caleb's earliest memories were the smells—summer flowers, frying fish. There was a stool, a chair, and a bed on which Francis slept. Caleb did not have his own bed, but a straw-stuffed mattress that he kept pushed beneath Francis's bed during the day and pulled out to the floor at night. Several times a year, Francis would rip open the mattress ticks and put in fresh straw. Caleb savored the nights after fresh straw was put in. It smelled good, like pleasant dreams.

Over the fireplace was a rack with Francis's cooking utensils, given to her by Mrs. Donaughby. On a wall rack by the door was Francis's rifle. She hunted rabbits to supplement the chickens and hogs they raised. Even with only one good eye, she was a fair shot. Caleb couldn't wait for the day when she would allow him to use the rifle.

On a small table was a bowl of walnuts and a

clay pot in which Francis put wildflowers to "brighten our home in honor of the goodness of the Lord." The pot was filled with blue chicory and orange daylilies. From the rafters hung braids of dried mint, sage, and bags of pine needles for tea. In the corners of the hut were barrels of potatoes and flour.

Caleb swept the floor, pushing the dirt out the door, then added small bits of wood to the fire. He dragged the braided rug outside and hung it over the garden fence and smacked the dust from it with the willow rug beater. Once the rug was back in place beside the bed, he went outside again to plant the raspberry bushes he'd collected that morning.

Caleb took the shovel and went into the garden. Unlike the rail-fenced garden by the Donaughby's farmhouse, the Jacobson's garden was surrounded with a barricade of tall piles of brush. This barricade was thick and practically impenetrable, and kept deer out of the vegetable rows. Every so often a rabbit would wriggle through the tight tangles, but Caleb would catch it and it would become a meal.

On the far side of the garden, Caleb leaned into the shovel, breaking the hard soil with its sharp tip. The earth he turned over was dry and crumbling. The next shovelful was darker, finer, and a wriggling grub within the soil twisted angrily, protesting its disturbance. Caleb dumped the soil to the side, and leaned in to the shovel once more.

With the first hole dug, he carefully placed the roots of the small raspberry bush in, filled the dirt around it, and tamped it down with his bare foot. Then he dug the second hole. He thought of the pies and cobblers his mother would make with the fruit next year. He wouldn't have to scour the farm for the berries as he'd always done.

When the last of the bushes was in place, Caleb watered each one with water from the rain barrel by the hut. He dipped the tin bucket into the deep maw of the barrel, coming up with sparkling liquid, taking a sip himself before returning to the garden to share with the newly-planted bushes. The sky was still heavy with gray clouds, but had yet to spare a single drop for the waiting creatures below. Caleb dropped the bucket on the ground and looked over the tall brush fence, licking the dry heat from his lips.

The field behind the Jacobson hut was the horse pasture. Adam Donaughby raised and sold the animals to farmers up and down the rolling road. The horses fascinated Caleb, and although he'd never been astride one, he imagined the power that would be there beneath him, and what it might feel like to cling to the silky mane as they galloped across a broad stretch of grass. Caleb liked to watch the horses as they grazed lazily or kicked up their heels against the wind. Sometimes when he was working in the garden, a horse would stray near the brush fence and Caleb would cluck to call it over. Caleb would run his fingers across the smooth coats, pull brambles from its mane, and blow gently on its face to make the horse nicker. Francis didn't approve of him touching the horses because they were valuable and it was with these animals that Mr. Donaughby made a fair income. Ten to twelve pounds a piece a good horse would bring.

Caleb glanced around to make sure his mother hadn't made a silent return, then clucked to a cluster of horses grazing not twenty yards away. All four looked up. Caleb knew these horses, as he did the twelve others, by name. Not names given by Mr. Donaughby, for the man did not see fit to call an animal with a name as one would a human being, but names Caleb had thought up himself.

"Ho there, Dandy!" said Caleb. "Come here!"

Dandy, a sorrel mare with a broad white blaze, ambled over to the brush fence. She reached out her muzzle for Caleb to rub. Sam, Star, and Thunder followed after, a dun, black, and gray respectively, and pushed their way past Dandy to receive scratchings.

"Watch there!" said Caleb as he stood on tip-toe and leaned carefully over the brush. "I'll pet each one." Several drips of water struck him on his bare shoulders and he lifted his face and said, "Look, we shall have our rain!"

The horses heard the distant sound before Caleb did, and they turned their heads around simultaneously, their ears pointed. Dandy shook her head. Sam stomped his hoof.

And then Caleb heard it, too. A screaming from across the pasture, down near the trees which lined the river.

"What . . . ?" he began, and the sound came again, shrill, pained. Not human, but agonized just the same.

Caleb raced from the garden, pausing just a moment to latch the small wooden gate. He cut across the backyard, past the outhouse, chicken pen, and the pig pen. The Jacobsons' three hogs grunted as he passed them, demanding to know why they had yet to be fed. Caleb climbed the rail fence and dropped into the horse pasture. He pulled himself aright and began to run.

The scream pierced the air again. All the horses

in the field had come to attention, standing with heads held high. But Dandy was drawn to the sound. She was well ahead of Caleb, trotting briskly to the far side of the field with her tail up like a silky flag. Caleb followed her, his feet pounding on the rough grass. The rain began to fall more seriously, and Caleb blinked drops from his eyelashes. He reached the edge of the field and slid down to the trees and the creek just beyond it. He skidded to a stop, and stared. Beside him, Dandy pawed at the earth and shook her head.

Along the banks of Wallace Creek were weeping willows, pines, and honey locust groves. Mr. Donaughby kept places along the creek cleared so the horses could drink, but there were also dense spots of vegetation so thick one could barely see into their depths. It was here, within a terrible tangle of locust trees, that the spotted two-year-old colt Caleb had named Flash had stumbled, and was now caught tight in an embrace of branches and thorns. He thrashed and kicked in an attempt to pull himself from the sharp barbs, but each struggle only tightened the trap as he sank into the creek-side muck left where the water had receded from the long spell of dry weather. His eyes were white with fear, his hide scraped and raw. He looked at Caleb and whinnied.

It was then that Caleb saw what had frightened Flash into the thorny trees. A nest of black snakes had been disturbed, and several were still visible beneath a rash of Virginia creepers. Dandy had spied the snakes too, and was pawing the earth as if trying to threaten them away.

Caleb ran back to where he could see the farmhouse in the distance. "Mr. Donaughby!" he shouted. The horses watched him, their hides twitching against the increasing intensity of the rain. "Mr. Donaughby, come! Help!"

He could not see the Quaker, but saw his wife, a black dress in the farmhouse yard, snatching wash from the line with the help of her daughters. "Mrs. Donaughby!" Caleb shouted, so loud the words scraped his throat.

The woman and her girls did not acknowledge the cry. They continued to pull sheets and blouses from the line, throw them into a basket, and then retreated into their cabin.

Caleb dug rainwater from his eyes and raced back down to the colt. Dandy pranced away down the creek to a place where she could take a drink, leaving Caleb with the bleeding animal. Flash trembled, lunged, and sank into the mud and thorns. There were new cuts on his hide, deep, gaping, red.

Caleb did not have a machete as Mr. Donaughby did, or even a knife. His mother considered him a child, and only under her supervision did she allow him to use sharp tools.

"If I could," Caleb said angrily, his fists clenching, "I would cut you free!"

The horse shivered and sank even deeper.

❧ 4 ❧

CALEB LOOKED INTO the eyes of the wounded animal, and for a moment felt as if he, himself, were caught in the thorns with his hide torn asunder. He had to do something. He raised his hand to the colt and said, "Ho there, now, calm."

The horse lifted a front hoof, and drove it down into the ground. He shook his head, and new cuts appeared on his neck where the thorns scraped him.

Caleb wiped his forehead. Sweat was mingled with the rain on his skin. He walked forward, very slowly, his hand still poised before him. He looked the colt in the eye, and said, "Ho. Shhh. Calm. Don't fight. Don't fight."

The horse watched him intently. Caleb could see tiny reflections of himself in the dark, wide eyes.

Caleb's fingers reached out, now mere inches from the animal's forelock. "Shh," he said. "Shhhhh." The horse seemed mesmerized by

Caleb's hand and voice, and went as still as a stone. Only the eyelashes trembled.

"Here now," said Caleb. His hand came down on the matted hair between the colt's ears. "Do not move. Hold still. If you don't struggle, I'll have you free."

The horse obeyed, and did not move.

With his free hand, Caleb began to snap away one thorny branch at a time, pulling it free from other branches and from the horse's hide, and throwing it far behind him. The rain swelled and grew heavy, soaking Caleb's trousers and running down his face in rivulets. Caleb snagged his palm on a large thorn, and it broke open and bled, but he continued to work at the branches.

Flash held perfectly still.

A voice, muffled in the downpour, came from above and behind. "What happens there! My good wife heard thee shout!"

It was Adam Donaughby, the Quaker.

"Colt's stuck, sir!" called Caleb without looking back. "Snakes frightened him!" Flash tossed his head at Caleb's shout, but went still again when Caleb finished speaking.

Mr. Donaughby's footsteps were heavy, and then the man was beside Caleb, his broad black hat knocked askew and dripping with rainwater, his bearded face set, his eyes narrowed. "Thee has a knife?"

"No, sir, only my hands," said Caleb.

"Move aside, then," said Mr. Donaughby, "I'll not have ye trampled by a colt mad with fear."

Caleb obeyed, backing away from the brush, but immediately the colt leapt up and tried to lash out with his front hoof. "I . . ." began Caleb, afraid to speak more. Adam Donaughby was a stern, serious man with whom Caleb had only had passing conversation. He knew it was wrong to correct elders, but the horse was at stake. "I think it best if I be with him. While you cut the branches."

Mr. Donaughby frowned. "No. Go thee now, before I have him free and he crush thee to the ground."

Caleb nodded. He took several more steps up the slope, but stopped as the horse began to thrash. Mr. Donaughby spoke easily, "Horse, horse," but to no avail. The horse would not be calmed. Mr. Donaughby looked up at Caleb, an expression of urgent confusion tugging his features. "What did thee do that he stayed still? Tell me quickly."

Caleb hesitated. "Talking," he said. "Touching him."

"Aye, touching him," said the man. "Touch him, then."

Caleb went to the colt and put his hand on the forelock. The colt let out a breath and stood still, his flanks fluttering only when Mr. Donaughby cut a barbed branch and pulled it from his hide. Caleb breathed slowly, pacing his with that of the horse, feeling, strangely, that for a moment they were one and the same.

"Let go now, boy!" said Mr. Donaughby. "Jump back!"

Caleb let go and leapt away. With a nicker and grunt, the colt bolted free of the locust trees, and galloped up the slope to the field.

"But he's hurt," said Caleb. "He's cut all about."

Mr. Donaughby nodded. "Yea, but he is free. I shall catch him now and have him to the stable to bind the wounds."

"Shall he live?" asked Caleb.

"God will decide," said Mr. Donaughby, tipping his head to let water run from his hat.

Caleb nodded.

Mr. Donaughby did not go then, but stood for a very long moment and looked at Caleb, his jaw set beneath the beard, his thick eyebrows a furious line that shadowed his dark eyes. Caleb suddenly realized he had done something terrible. He had come into the horse pasture without permission. Perhaps Mr. Donaughby thought he'd made things worse by trying to release Flash on his own. Caleb shivered, and the rain felt suddenly very cold.

Then, without a word, Mr. Donaughby turned and walked away with long, determined strides, up the slope to the horse pasture, and disappeared from sight.

"Dandy," Caleb called, his voice trembling. The mare was still down the river, having finished drinking and now tugging stinkweed from the bank with her teeth. She looked up, green dangling from her lips. "I'm in trouble."

Dandy went to grazing again. Caleb climbed the slope and trudged across the horse pasture to his cottage. The rain was lightening into a mist, and gnats had come out from the weeds in full force. Caleb slapped away the bothersome insects. On the far side of the field, he could see Mr. Donaughby coming from his stable with a length of rope. He would find Flash and take him in, apply salve, and hope for the best. Beyond the stable, the women of the Donaughby family as well as Francis Jacobson were back outside, cutting weeds in the garden. In unison the four daughters looked up at Caleb then back down again at their chore. The oldest daughter, Charity, put her hands on her hips as if scolding him. Caleb wondered what they were thinking of the boy who disobeyed their father's rules.

Back in the hut, Caleb tugged off his wet breeches and hung them on a wall hook near the fire. He sat naked on the stool, and crossed his arms. His toes wriggled back and forth against the splintery wood of the floor. "I'm in trouble deep," he said aloud. He was supposed to be chopping potatoes for the pigs. He was supposed to be practicing his letters. But he couldn't move. What would Mr. Donaughby do? Would he make them leave the farm? Would Caleb be beaten?

At long last, Caleb dragged his stool to the table, moved the jar of flowers aside, and took his slate for its place on the wall shelf with the bowls. The Jacobsons rarely had paper, much less ink powder, except for special times when they sold a hog or when Mrs. Donaughby paid Caleb for collecting sacks of chokecherries. Bits of chalk were easy to find along the creek, and it was with this that Caleb practiced his writing and his arithmetic.

His hand still shaking, he wrote his ABCs, working to form them the way they looked on Mrs. Donaughby's hornbooks. Even though Caleb had only begun attending the Quaker school the previous fall, before he turned six in December, he had learned his letters and numbers quickly. He could now write whole passages from the Bible from memory.

"The Lord is my sheperd I shall not want," he wrote. It made him feel better to write. Not just the phrases he chose, but the feeling of wonder that his hand was forming something of meaning.

He looked at the words. He wished he could write his own words, his own thoughts, like King

David had written these so long ago. But Mrs. Donaughby said wanting to write one's own thoughts so early in their schooling was vain. "In the beginning God creted the hevens and the earth," Caleb wrote. "For God so loved the world he sent his only begoten son." After each passage, Caleb looked at it for a moment, then wiped the words away with the side of his hand. If he'd written the Bible, he wondered what he would have said.

"Horse," he wrote. He knew that word, because Mrs. Donaughby had taught the boys how to write it the last day of lessons in May, along with "cattle," "sheep," and "farm." But Caleb didn't know the words to tell of his misadventure with Flash. So he drew a horse in the brambles, and a chalky, featureless boy standing beside him. Caleb looked at this, then quickly wiped away the scene of his crime.

By the time Francis could be seen coming up the pathway across the cattle field, Caleb had gotten back into his now dried breeches, fed the chickens and pigs, and had added cedar chips to the fire. He quickly sat on his mother's bed and began weaving on his tape-loom. Idle hands were of the old deluder Satan, and Francis would have none of it. On this simple handheld loom Caleb could weave garters and breeches suspenders, or for his mother, gloves or hair ties. Often he made braids to tie beans or to hang foods from the ceiling beams. Today, with wool combed and donated to the Jacobsons from the Donaughbys, Caleb began some bonnet strings for Francis. Those on her bonnet now were frayed. Maybe a gift would make his crime less terrible.

Caleb's mother appeared at the open front door, her shawl still glistening damp from the earlier rain. Under her arm was a loaf of bread wrapped in a towel. She removed her shoes carefully and placed them just inside the door so as not to track mud on the floor Caleb had swept. Her bonnet and shawl went on a nail on the wall.

"Good day, Mother," said Caleb.

"Mrs. Donaughby had extra bread today from our baking," Francis said, moving to sit on the chair at the table, then bending to rub her ankles.

"That was kind."

She sighed heavily and stretched her shoulders. "The baby Prudence is no better. Teeth are coming in poorly. Dear little thing, crying and fussing, hot as a poker in the fire. We'll pray God brings her good health soon."

Caleb said, "Yes'am."

Then Francis looked at Caleb. "Mister Donaughby said he needed to come here in the morning. To speak with us."

Caleb's heart jumped. "Oh?"

"Indeed," said Francis.

"Why?"

"I do not know," said his mother. She rubbed her good eye, then her neck. Sometimes her body ached, but she rarely complained. Life was full of pains and sadness, but the Lord expected his servants to accept them cheerfully.

"Am I in trouble?"

"Would you be in trouble? Have you done something for which you will be punished?"

Caleb's voice was soft. "I . . . I think not. I can't remember. I don't think so."

Francis watched him for a moment, then said, "All right, boy. I'm sure that you haven't. Back to your work." Francis got up to stir the stew. Caleb returned to his weaving.

Maybe Mr. Donaughby is coming tomorrow to offer to buy our piglets, Caleb thought. *Maybe he needs more chokecherries, or wants me to collect birch twigs so his wife can make new baking whisks.*

Dinner was the pork and potatoes from the pot, cold this time, and tasty with a thin layer of lard which Caleb slathered on a slice of hard bread. Caleb found a piece of gristle in his pork, and pushed it to the side of his mouth so later, he could have something good on which to chew.

The night settled softly, with another misting of rain that pattered the roof of the hut and made the air outside the door smell fresh and clean. There was a leaking spot in the ceiling, and Francis put a bowl beneath to catch the drips. "I'll climb up on the roof and patch that in the morning," Caleb offered.

Francis lit a candle on the table, and by its light and the low glow of the fire in the hearth, she went to sewing a new a blouse for herself with a leftover piece of linen Mrs. Donaughby had given her several weeks ago. Caleb continued with his tape-loom. His thoughts drifted like smoke from the colt to Mr. Donaughby's stern face to the daughters who watched him so silently and seriously from over the fence. He knew the daughters' names—Charity, the eldest at seven, and then Patience, Humility, Faith, and the baby Prudence, who was just a year. Yet he never talked to them, nor they to him. He encountered them only at the solemn Sunday worship services in the farmhouse, to which Caleb and his mother were welcomed. Sometimes, as in the Quaker tradition, the daughters would be moved by the spirit and would say something about God's love. But they never spoke directly to Caleb.

Caleb paused in his weaving. "Mother, what're girls for? They rarely say a word. They don't laugh. They don't go fishing. They don't run or roll in the grass."

Francis reached over from her chair to hug her son. Her good eye sparkled. "Caleb, Quaker girls, as are girls in other families, are to be obedient and quiet. They learn housewifery and such to get on in life. You won't see them caring for anything else, for it would be a waste of time."

Caleb huffed, and he wove more of the yarn. The bonnet ties were growing quickly and dangled nearly to the floor. "If I was a girl, would I have to behave such?"

"I'd teach you differently than I do now."

"I wouldn't be allowed to fish or tell jokes?"

"Caleb, you think too much."

"What empty heads girls have, with no thoughts of fun."

"That isn't so," said Francis. "But ideas which don't fit with a woman's life must be put aside. Just as ideas which do not fit our religious beliefs must be cast away. Or thoughts which do not fit with a black's life must be put aside. To prevent tragedies."

"What tragedies?"

Francis hesitated. "On this farm you're a free boy."

"Yes'am," said Caleb. "We're free. We have papers. I can't read but you told me what they say."

Francis could not read herself, but her master in New York had read the papers to her as she had been freed, and Francis had the words memorized.

"Yes," said Caleb's mother slowly. "But hear me.

You're treated like an equal here, and the good Lord knows you should be treated such anywhere in this world. But that's not the way it is. The way things should be and the way they are don't always meet. Sometimes they're so far apart they can't even see each other."

Caleb scratched his nose and frowned, staring into the glowing fireplace as a dried leaf caught fire and sizzled.

Francis continued, "I don't allow you off the property. But you've seen the black men rolling hogsheads past the farm, followed by white men with whips."

Caleb nodded.

"And," said Francis, "you've seen folks come to the Donaughby farm to buy a horse or to visit. They're not all Quakers. You've seen the difference in their dress? Their bright colors? Their silver buttons and lace sleeves?"

"Yes'am."

"These white folks respect the Donaughbys' views, but I've seen their faces when they notice you."

Caleb had seen their faces, too, and he'd always stayed out of their way as his mother had demanded. But Caleb had never wondered why. It seemed to him that most adults just didn't care for children who weren't their own.

"Someday," said Francis, "you'll travel from this farm. You'll find things I wish I could keep from you. You'll see most black people are not free but are slaves. As I was once. That day's coming as sure as a storm in the spring. I can feel it. But I fear it, Lord knows I do."

Caleb opened his mouth to ask his mother what it was like when she was a slave, but suddenly she threw up a hand. "Oh!" she said. "It's late! Bedtime's come and gone. We've much to do tomorrow. Let's say our prayers and be to bed."

The knitting and weaving were put aside. Francis blew out the candle. Caleb took to the floor on his knees for his prayers, and then to his mattress for sleep. His mother said her prayers as well, then climbed onto her bed. Not long after, Caleb could hear her snoring. He stared at the walls, at the dancing glow-horses on the wood, moving up and down and in and out of the seams of the logs. He thought of himself riding Dandy over a field to rescue a herd of horses caught in thorny brambles.

Mr. Donaughby is coming tomorrow.

The thought came like a slap. He prayed softly, "God, don't let me be in trouble. Don't let me be in . . ."

A knock awoke Caleb from deep sleep, and he rubbed his eyes in the dim light of early dawn. He clambered from his mattress to see who was there. Mr. Donaughby stood in the cabin doorway, his hat set squarely on his head, his fingertips pressed together. He said, "We must talk."

Caleb's stomach clenched.

"But first, I must speak with thy mother."

I'm in trouble for Flash and his cut-up hide! Flash has died, and now I owe him money! I have no money! Tears sprang to Caleb's eyes, and he dug them out furiously. Being in trouble was bad enough, letting the stern man see him cry was worse. He looked away, his vision blurred.

"Call thy mother," said Mr. Donaughby.

But Caleb didn't have to. Francis was already up at the sound of voices, wrapping herself modestly in a shawl and pushing a piece of hair behind her

ear. She shuffled to the door. "Caleb, you're crying?" she asked. And then, "Sir?"

Mr. Donaughby cleared his throat. "I have
watched thy boy with my horses, Mistress Jacobson.
I have seen the way the mares come to him at your
garden fence. I have seen the way the stallions
stand at attention when he speaks."

Caleb stopped digging at his tears. Mr. Donaughby had seen him with the horses at other
times? This was much worse than just one time
with the colt! Mr. Donaughby would banish them
like Adam and Eve had been banished from the
Garden!

"I . . ." began Caleb.

"Hush!" said Francis. "Mr. Donaughby, sir,
please?"

Mr. Donaughby coughed. Then he said, "Thy
boy has been blessed with this talent at a tender
age, yet a talent is not to be wasted nor hidden
under a bushel, as the Good Book says. Horses
calm around him. Even a colt, caught in a thicket
and mad with pain went silent with thy son's
touch."

"I see," said Francis.

"I came to request permission for thy son to accompany me to River's Pine to take a pair of skit-
tish yearlings."

Caleb looked at his mother. She was standing
straight, and the fist holding her shawl closed was
tight, but there was a slight twitching at the corner
of her mouth, as if there was something she
wanted to say but couldn't. Caleb found himself
counting silently to himself, wondering how long
it would be until someone said something.

And then Francis took a breath and said, "Of
course, sir. You have confidence in my child, thank

you, sir. But a moment, that I might dress him properly for such a venture?"

Mr. Donaughby nodded. "I shall leave in but a quarter hour." And he turned and strode toward his farmhouse.

Caleb's heart pounded as his mother scrubbed his face with a skin-searing vigor. He was going off the farm! What would he see? Who would he meet? As he ran back and forth between the door and the table, his mother stitched a hole in his shirt and tied up a napkin with cheese and bread.

"Mama!" he moaned when she insisted they say a prayer before he went. But Francis was not to be argued with, and the two of them knelt on the floor by the fireplace.

"Our dear Lord Jesus," Francis prayed. It was all Caleb could do to keep his eyes shut. "I knew this time was coming. I felt it in my blood and in my heart. Protect Caleb from all evil. Thy will be done. Amen."

Evil and harm? What evil and harm could there be? Mr. Donaughby had a hunting rifle to shoot bears or wolves if any should try to come after them. Caleb said "Amen," jumped up and raced out of the hut.

"Caleb, wait!"

Exasperated, Caleb spun around. "What?"

"You must take this," his mother said. She tucked his freeman's paper carefully into the front of his shirt. "In case something happens to Mr. Donaughby you will have this. And hear me, son." Her voice was stern and anxious. "You don't speak unless you are spoken to. I've been to River's Pine. Once in my life, passing through, before I was taken in by the Donaughbys. You must do as I say and be silent!"

And with a pat on his head, she sent him running across the field with the napkin of food to where Mr. Donaughby was tying the frantic yearlings to the rear of his wagon.

5

"THEE ARE NOT to speak unless requested," Mr. Donaughby said as they rattled down the rolling road in the wagon with the gelding Caleb had named Puddle at the harness and the two dappled yearlings tied to the rear. Mr. Donaughby had bid Caleb sit in back and mind the colts. "I am allowing thee to accompany me because thee has a soothing affect on animals. But that aside, thee will keep silent."

Caleb put his elbows on the seat beside Mr. Donaughby. He could smell damp dirt on the road from the previous night's rain. He could see rabbits in the brush at the forest's edge. He could hear the nervous hoof steps of the yearlings.

Curiosity got the best of Caleb, and he asked, "Why, sir, can't I speak? There might be a great deal to say. I've never been off the farm nor traveled in a wagon and . . ."

Mr. Donaughby pulled Puddle up short and turned to look at Caleb. His eyes were steady beneath the heavy brows and broad hat. "Thou have had run of my land ever since thee was born. But it is time thee learned that my farm isn't the world, and the world doesn't fancy Negroes. I say this to be generous. Does thou understand?"

"No, sir."

"Then just let it be that thou say nothing. It is best for those we encounter to think thou art my property. A Quaker should own neither man nor child, nay, a man of any faith should own neither man nor child. Yet it would fare better if, when off my land, you art seen as mine."

"But," Caleb straightened up. "I belong to Mama, sir!"

Mr. Donaughby slapped the reins against Puddle's back, urging the horse to move ahead. "Silence."

Caleb sat back down on the hard wagon bed and watched the new world roll by. Occasionally, when the grass at roadside was tall and close enough, he would pull some free and hold it to the yearlings. As they nibbled the sticky green blades, their minds seemed to be taken off the journey.

Half an hour later, there came in view around a bend a large building of questionable sturdiness and questionable purpose. Caleb gazed from his knees. The building was weather-worn and seemed to lean unsteadily on its foundation. It was two stories tall, made of dark wood, and with many shuttered windows. There was a sign above the front door, and Caleb's mind scrambled to decipher the words painted on it. "K-I-N-G-S C-R-O-W-N T-A-V-E-R-N." Beneath the letters was a painting of a crown through which a unicorn and lion jumped.

Posts with tarnished rings had been planted by the road outside the tavern's front door. Saddled horses were tethered to them. The animals stood with heads down, switching flies and pawing at the ground. On the wall of the tavern were large sheets of paper, advertising items and making pronouncements Caleb could barely see from the wagon, let alone read for their complex words.

At the side of the tavern, separated by a good thirty feet, was a raised platform. Behind the platform were lean-tos filled with chicken and duck coops. Milling about the platform and lean-tos was a cluster of white men tending small herds of sheep and goats with sticks and dogs. The screeching and bleating of the animals was ear-piercing.

Caleb ached to ask Mr. Donaughby about the place before they rode past it, but to Caleb's surprise, Mr. Donaughby drew Puddle up beside the tavern, pulled back the hand brake, and climbed down.

"I'll be but a moment," he said.

Caleb watched for several long moments after Mr. Donaughby was gone. A sense of unease fell over him, and he pulled back from the wagon's edge. He didn't know where he was. He was alone.

Caleb remembered his mother's warnings the day before. What if a bear came after him, or a wolf? What if something even worse snatched him away? Caleb looked anxiously at the men with the livestock. They wouldn't care if a bear came for him and carried him off, or something worse.

The colts at the back of the wagon shook their halters and tugged at the rope. Caleb crawled back to them and stroked their ears, saying, "It's all right," calming them but not himself. He listened above the noises of the people and animals to see if a wolf might be howling in the woods.

A horse and rider came up the road from the other direction, moving at a steady clip. The horse was a large gray mount. It held its head up confidently. The rider was a tall man in a light-colored broadcloth cloak, tall leather boots, and dark broad-brimmed hat. He had an air of quiet dignity, and when he drew his horse up to a tethering post, he looked directly at Caleb in the wagon.

It was then Caleb saw the man was black.

Caleb stared, forgetting the wolf momentarily. He had never seen a black man riding a horse before. The only black men he'd seen had been pushing hogsheads, driving oxen, or trailing behind white men in ropes.

The man dismounted, tied his horse, then strolled toward the gathering at the platform. When he passed by the wagon he nodded, smiled, and said, "Good morning, son."

Caleb opened his mouth but shut it again. He had been told by his mother and Mr. Donaughby to say nothing.

The man stopped yards short of the white men, not seeming afraid, but seeming to be more comfortable out of their midst. He rubbed his chin and watched the goats and sheep intently. Caleb watched the man with the same intensity.

"Then now." It was Mr. Donaughby, climbing back into the wagon. Caleb hadn't seen him coming, and he flinched at the voice. "I've what I need, and we are off for River's Pine." Mr. Donaughby put a small, cloth-wrapped bundle on the seat beside him, then reached down to release the brake. He noticed Caleb watching the men around the platform, and said, "That is an auction. Men bring animals for sale, and sometimes the tavern owner sells items he's had shipped from abroad. Fine English items. Dishes, fabric, and such."

As Mr. Donaughby picked up the reins, the well-dressed black man looked over, raised one hand, and said, "Mr. Donaughby, sir. Good day."

Mr. Donaughby nodded. "Mr. Banneker. Thee have come for the auction? It is quite a journey for thee I would think."

"I've thoughts of adding new stock to my sheep," said Mr. Banneker. "I hope to find some here. And thee?"

"I've business up the road at River's Pine."

"A fair journey to thee, then, and to the boy. And bid your fine wife good health on thy return."

Mr. Donaughby nodded. "And good health to thy mother," he said. And then the wagon was off with a jerk, Puddle picking up a slow trot, and the yearlings tossing their heads and fighting until Caleb reached back to them to calm them.

A good while later, Mr. Donaughby steered Puddle across a rattley wooden bridge and onto a long, treelined lane. The lane took them past a cattle pasture, a meadow tilled and spotted with rows of bright green corn plants, and through a huge field in which broad-leaved plants grew in rows and in which sweat-slicked, shirtless black men and bent-backed black women wielded picks and hoes. The lane then divided, with the left fork leading to a collection of buildings and the right fork continuing up a hill to a large white house. Caleb stared. He had never seen so many people. He wondered if this was a town. His mother had told him about towns.

The wagon took the left fork and stopped in front of the first building. Caleb could see inside. There was a devilish glow from a huge brick oven, and a loud and rhythmic pinging of hammers. The fire was reflected on the faces of the men who swung the hammers and stoked the fire. A horsefly bit Caleb on the neck and he slapped it away.

"Thee must wait here." Mr. Donaughby climbed from the wagon, brushing his breeches and read-justing his hat.

Next to the fire-filled shop was a barn and pad-docks, much like the ones back at Mr. Don-aughby's farm. Black men moved in and out, hauling bales of hay and straw in, rolling wheel-barrows of muck out, and making repairs on a damaged fence of one of three small paddocks.

Across the lane from the barn was a low-roofed shed. Outside it sat dark-skinned children, scrap-ing the meat from deer, bear, and fox hides. Dry-ing leather was hung on racks, stretched out tight and wide. Up the lane were tall, narrow sheds in which Caleb could see dried leaves hanging from rafters. Huge barrels—the hogsheads—sat along the outer walls. And, barely visible much farther along the lane, past a grove of apple trees, with only roofs and stone chimneys showing above a rise in the lane, was a cluster of cabins.

Caleb waved at a black boy who was wheeling a load of dirty straw from the paddock to dump on a compost pile. The boy glanced up but did not return the wave.

"Adam Donaughby, sir!" came a booming voice from the doorway of the barn, and out strode a very round, very pale man with a riding crop in his hand. His head wobbled as he walked, and his chin was tilted upward as if he thought himself fancy, yet he was much too oily and dirty to be such. He dressed in silk stockings, breeches, velvet waistcoat, leather shoes with silver buckles, leather mitts, and a tri-cornered hat. But the buttons of the coat didn't quite meet, and the white shirt beneath boasted a brown stain that looked like a smudge of horse manure.

Mr. Donaughby said, "Good morning, Mr. Whitley," but did not bow nor remove his hat to the man. Only God could bring the hat from the head of a Quaker.

"Have you ever thought of fighting cocks, Mr. Donaughby?" asked the fat man with a huge grin. "A sport that has of late caught my fancy. I'd fought dogs until April, but I just couldn't breed the fire into them that is necessary for a successful row. Fighting cocks, however, they are quick and brutal!" He wiped his nose with one mitt-covered hand, and it left a red streak. "Oh," the man continued, "but no, Quakers wouldn't stand for it, eh?"

Two black men emerged from the barn, one carrying a struggling multicolored rooster and the other bearing three dead, bloodied roosters, their necks swinging, their dead little eyes dulled. The live bird was taken to a coop beside the barn. Mr. Whitley called to the man with the dead birds, "You've got supper there. I am a generous master, indeed!"

The man with the dead birds bowed and said, "Yes, Master Whitley, thank you sir," and then hastened up the lane, past the apple grove, then down toward the rows of cabins.

Mr. Donaughby ignored the roosters. "I've brought the yearlings thee chose from my stock two weeks ago. I pray thee will find them to thy liking. They are trained to halter and ready to begin formal schooling."

"Fine," said Mr. Whitley. "I'm certain I shall find them in excellent health. I am anxious to break them into racing animals. I was in Baltimore a fortnight ago, and heard a man say, 'Marylanders do so love their horses. If they were to attend church five miles away, and their horses were in a field eight miles away, they would walk the eight to ride the five!' "

Mr. Donaughby nodded. "Aside from a pouch of coins in a Marylander's pocket or a riverside warehouse full of tobacco, he sees a good horse as his most valuable possession. Next to his good wife, of course."

"Of course," said Mr. Whitley. "Or his slave cabins full of black studs!" Mr. Whitley laughed loud and harsh, but Mr. Donaughby's smile vanished, and he stood silently with his arms stiffly at his side until Mr. Whitley was done.

Then Mr. Whitley said, "Before we discuss business, sir, would you first honor me by joining me at the house for a bit of refreshment? Mrs. Whitley would be most upset if I didn't extend hospitality and give you a comfortable chair and a bite of honey cake. Horses and blackies have no notion of time, and we can enjoy the air from the porch."

Caleb could see a slight hesitation in Mr. Donaughby's face, but then he said, "Thee are most kind, Mr. Whitley. We shall put the yearlings into thy paddock and they will be ready for thy inspection at thy pleasure."

Caleb knew this was his cue. He clambered from the back of the wagon and began to untie the first of the yearlings. But suddenly, there was a whistle through the air and a sharp, cutting pain on his shoulder.

"Oww!" Caleb cried, dropping the rope. He looked up to see Mr. Whitley scowling, his riding crop held aloft. The man's face was twisted in a dreadful, frightful sneer.

6

CALEB TOOK A stumbling step backward, stunned by the blow of the white man's crop. The yearling he'd been holding pranced and snorted, and Caleb grabbed up the lead rope so the animal wouldn't dash off.

But again Mr. Whitley snapped the crop, bringing the braided leather into Caleb's wrist. Again Caleb dropped the rope, and this time the horse bolted a good thirty feet to stand and stare with its hide trembling. Caleb's fists drew up, and he was ready to lunge at the man but Mr. Donaughby grabbed him by the upper arm and held him still.

"No black pup touches my animals without my permission!" Mr. Whitley snarled, spit flying from his lips. "Mr. Donaughby, have you no control over your Negro?"

"Caleb," said Mr. Donaughby. Caleb struggled but Mr. Donaughby was much stronger than he could have expected, and Caleb couldn't free himself. "Caleb, hear me. We may not need thy help after all. Back into the wagon with thee."

"But . . . !"

"Silence." Mr. Donaughby let go of Caleb then, and Caleb clutched the wounded spot on his shoulder and wrist, feeling at once the deep, sharp sting of split flesh, the warm flow of blood through his shirt, and the flush of embarrassment as the black men nearby glanced his way.

What had he done wrong? Why didn't Mr. Donaughby tell Mr. Whitley he had no call to whip him?

I didn't do anything wrong!

Mr. Whitley slid his crop into the side of his boot, leaving the handle out so, Caleb guessed, he could get it again easily. Then Mr. Whitley shouted, "Gaddi!" The boy with the wheelbarrow put it aside and hurried over.

"Yes, sir, Master Whitley?"

"Get these horses to the large paddock. Make sure they have hay and water, and latch that gate tightly or I'll have your hide, do you understand me?"

"Yes, Master Whitley," said the boy. Caleb saw that the boy watched the ground when he spoke. He even kept his head down as he unhitched the second animal from the wagon, then slowly approached the one who had bolted.

"Fine animals," said Mr. Whitley. "I like spirit!"

It was with angry pride that Caleb saw the yearling who had run off try to bolt again as the black boy stepped on the lead to snatch it up. Both colts fought him as he led them to the paddock. Mr. Donaughby should have told Mr. Whitley that Caleb was good with horses and they liked him.

But Mr. Donaughby said nothing. He and Mr. Whitley walked between the barn and the blacksmith shop, then up the lane toward the big, white house on the hill.

When the men were far enough away that he was certain they couldn't hear, Caleb said, "I did nothing wrong!" Huge tears burned his vision, and his body began to shake.

"What's this? You cryin', boy?"

Caleb dug at his eyes with the heels of his hands and looked up. There stood the older boy who had put the horses into the paddock. He was tall and gangly, with close-cropped hair and dark skin. He had no shirt or shoes. His trousers were worn thin. Wrapped around the palms of his hands were crusted rags, worn there like work gloves, Caleb guessed.

"No," said Caleb.

"Why's your face all wet?"

"My face isn't wet. Just sweat, that's all."

"What's your name, boy?"

"Caleb Jacobson."

One of the boy's eyebrows went up. "You got a surname?"

"A surname? What's that?"

"You said Caleb Jacobson. How you get a second name?"

Caleb shrugged. "Mama gave it to me."

"Jacob your daddy's name?"

"Mama never told me my daddy's name."

"Your daddy dead?"

"Yes. He died saving a man from drowning in New York. My daddy was a hero."

The older boy rolled his eyes. "I think you're telling a fib. Maybe your daddy just got sold off. Or maybe he's a mad man running loose in the woods!"

Caleb felt himself straighten up. This boy was

poking fun at him, and he wouldn't have it. "He's not a madman!"

"Maybe he is."

Caleb took a breath. He didn't know what to say next.

"My name's Gaddi," said the boy. "How old are you?"

"Six. Born Christmas Day in '59."

"Well, I'm almost eleven. Mostly a man."

"Why that fat man hit me?" Caleb asked, glancing at the white house on the hill. Mr. Whitley and Mr. Donaughby were nearing the steps, and a woman in a dress with a wide skirt was greeting them with a sweep of her arms. "I should have hit him back! I don't care mama say no fighting!"

Gaddi's eyes widened, and he looked both ways as if he was afraid someone might have heard. But the other folks just kept at their tasks—pounding the anvils, scraping the hides, driving nails into the boards of the paddock fence. "Hush!" said the boy. "Master Whitley has owl's ears! He may be in his house, he may be by the river with a fishin' pole, he may even be ridin' to Baltimore, but that don't mean he can't hear every whisper we make."

"He's not God, is he?"

"Maybe he is, and maybe he ain't."

Caleb's fists balled up. His heart pounded with renewed indignation. "I didn't do anything wrong! Mr. Donaughby brought me to handle the colts, and I got smacked for it!"

"I can't believe your squallin'! You never been hit?"

"Not for nothing. Mama swats me for not listening."

"A swat?" The older boy shook his head in disbelief. "What about your master, don't he hit none?"

"I don't have a master, just my mama."

"You mean to say you's a free boy?"

"Yes."

"Well! I never met no free boy before. Where you live?"

"Quality and Quantity, the Donaughby farm, up the road."

"Who the Donaughbys?"

"The Quakers. That man that brought me here."

"Quakers, no wonder. Well, Caleb, son of the crazy man in the woods, like a mouse watches the sky for a hawk, you best watch the sky for Master's crop."

Caleb kicked a clump of dirt, sending it in a spray. "But I'm supposed to help with the yearlings!"

"Quit piping. You supposed to do what Mr. Whitley says." Then, he took a long breath and said, "Listen, boy. You sit in the back of that wagon and don't go nowhere, and I'll bring you something to eat later. How's that sound?"

"I've got food," Caleb said.

Gaddi said, "Fine, then, you don't need anything!"

Caleb suddenly didn't want the boy to think ill of him. He said, "I've got nothing to drink. Have you got water?"

Gaddi let out a long breath. He said, "Get in the wagon. You be quiet and I'll bring water when I can."

Caleb climbed into the wagon and drew his knees up. As Gaddi turned to leave, Caleb was startled to see long, ugly scars across the boy's bare back. There were raised stripes and deep gashes. Were these the work of Mr. Whitley's crop?

Caleb took off his own shirt and examined the damage on his shoulder and wrist. It wasn't as bad as he'd thought, but there were indeed splits in the skin, and they were just now growing tacky enough to stop bleeding. "Mama won't stand for this," Caleb told himself, but he knew that would not change a thing. It had happened, and that was that.

For a long while, as the May sun crawled across the cloudless sky, Caleb watched the men in the shops and the people in the fields. There were not only men and women bending over in the rows, but young children, too, scattered across the field, hurling stones into baskets, as several men with whips watched from horseback.

"I don't like this place," Caleb said to himself around a piece of cheese. "One day, that old fat man is gonna know it's wrong to hit people."

It seemed like forever before Gaddi returned with a tin cup of cold water in his hands. "Thank you," Caleb said.

Gaddi said nothing but picked up the handles of his wheelbarrow and went back inside the barn.

And Caleb felt lonely and forgotten for the first time in his life.

They returned to Quality and Quantity in the mid-afternoon, when the scorching sun was high in the sky and the hard-packed earth, needing yet another drenching of rain, was beginning to split open once more.

The wagon pulled up to the stable behind the farmhouse, Puddle prancing the last yards as though he were happy to be home. Mr. Donaughby, seeming exhausted, muttered, "Hang up the halters, boy," then walked toward the farmhouse with the package he'd gotten at the tavern.

Caleb draped the halters over his shoulder and took them into the stable. He paused just inside the wide door and glanced around. He'd never been inside this place before, but he liked the feel of it. It smelled of fresh hay and horses, and the shadows were cool and pleasant. A row of wooden pegs on a beam near the center of the stable was strung with bridles, ropes, and halters. Caleb added the ones he carried to them, then turned to leave.

"Hello," came a soft voice from one of the stalls.

Caleb, startled, whirled about toward the sound. There, with a rake in hand, was Charity Donaughby. Her black dress and black bonnet were covered in straw dust. Her straw-colored hair curled from beneath the bonnet like feathers.

"Hello," said Caleb.

"Did thee sell the yearlings to Mr. Whitley?"

"Yes."

"Did my father get the necklace from the tavern?"

"Necklace?" He felt strange talking to a girl. He wondered if he was supposed to. He didn't need any more chances to be in trouble.

Charity nodded. "An Anodyne necklace. For Prudence. Her teeth are coming in badly. The necklace is for healing her. We've tried rue juice in her ear, and teaberry root on her gums, but neither helped. Poor child, she is hurting so."

"Ah," said Caleb. He scratched his head and kicked at a stray flake of hay on the dirt floor. "I'm sorry."

"Yes," said Charity. And then Caleb could see

the tremble of her lip. "She might die."

"Oh," he said. Francis had told him the baby Prudence was very sick with her teeth. But Caleb hadn't thought much of it. He'd only seen the baby in passing, and didn't know her. He felt sorry for Charity suddenly.

"I'm being punished for crying during Scriptures this morning. We are all sad and praying for her health. But I wasn't to cry as Father read from the Good Book. So I've been put to cleaning stalls as well as my other chores."

Caleb didn't know what to say. This was a girl, who had no thoughts of fun or play and never rolled in the grass.

"I'll pray for your sister," he offered.

Charity rubbed her eyes. "I thank thee."

"The yearlings brought a good price."

"Father will be pleased," said Charity. "He said evening last that thee has a way with the beasts. He said thee has a gift from God."

"Yes," said Caleb. He looked over his shoulder. He didn't want to be caught talking to the girl lest he find himself doing extra chores as well.

"You saw the plantation, River's Pine. Was it lovely?"

In Caleb's mind he saw the stripes across Gaddi's back and the pomposity of the piggish Mr. Whitley as he waved his riding crop. The sweating men, women, and children in the field, looked over by a man with a whip. The dead roosters. The huge white house on the hill, far enough away from the sweating black bodies to not smell them, like some of the fancy ladies who visited the Donaughby farm on occasion and held handkerchiefs to their noses when Caleb was close. His shoulder began to sting again, where he'd been struck. He was afraid Charity might see the bit of blood that had seeped through the back of his shirt.

"I didn't like it much," he admitted.

Charity propped the rake against the stall door, and came out into the aisle. She shook her bonnet and dusted her dress off with her hands. "Why not?" Her face was as pale as a whitened pebble, and curious as a kitten he'd once owned.

Caleb lowered his voice. If Mr. Donaughby had ears like Gaddi said Mr. Whitley had, he would be able to hear Caleb's complaints clear to the farmhouse. "I just didn't."

"Oh." Charity sounded disappointed. "I've never been away from our farm. I've always thought it would be fine, to go off on a long, long ride. To see new places and people."

"Well," said Caleb. He didn't know more to say, or if he should. "Good afternoon, then."

Charity said, "Good afternoon, Caleb."

Caleb was surprised to hear her say his name. He was surprised she knew his name. She was one of the Donaughby daughters who stayed in their yard or house and never sang or yelled out loud. He didn't think girls knew anything but hanging laundry and hoeing weeds.

The walk down the path seemed longer today. His mother would ask about his trip. But if he told the truth, it would make her sad, or angry, and he might not be allowed to go with Mr. Donaughby again. And even though he had stinging shoulders to show for his travels today, he wanted to see more of Maryland. He wanted to meet more people like Gaddi.

"Caleb!" His mother was at the door, waving a rag in her hand. Caleb raised his hand in return, and ran into her warm arms. She held him as if

he had been missing but now was found, like the
boy in the Bible story. Then she scurried him inside and served him fried potatoes and a slice of
bread.

He gobbled up the food, hanging his head over
the bowl. Usually, Francis was particular about his
table manners. But this afternoon, she let him be.

When the meal was over, Caleb took off his shirt
and prepared to go outside to feed the pigs and
water the raspberries. But his mother stopped him
with a touch on his arm. "Caleb," she said. "How
was your journey?"

Caleb looked at her face, at the worry and hope
within.

"There is a mark on your shoulder and wrist,"
she said.

For a moment Caleb thought of saying he'd
fallen in thistles, but she would know it was a lie.
She sensed what he had seen, what he had expe-
rienced. She understood that he was a different
boy now than when he'd left in the morning.

And so, he just shrugged, pulled away gently,
and walked through the shimmering heat to the
garden.

Later that day three things occurred. Another
rain storm came, and heavily. Baby Prudence Donaughby died with her bad teeth. And Mr. Donaughby asked Francis if Caleb could continue to
help him with his horses as an apprentice.

❧ 7 ❧

April 19, 1770

We went north yestrday to a cabin in the forest. A nice farmer named Mr. Albert Conner had bot a horse from Mr. Donaughby but the horse has turned wilde. Mr. Conner sent for Mr. Donaughby to tran the filly again or return payment. We collected the filly and brought her back. I shall help Mr. Donaughby tran her again. She is gentil with me and will not bitte. Mr. Donaughby says she went wilde becaus Mr. Conner's son treted her poorley. When we took her to Mr. Conner last month, she was docul. Most creatures rebel against crool treatment, Mr. Donaughby said to me.

While at the farm Mr. Conner spoke much about his anger for the tax laws of King George. He said he is weery of the tenson. He feels the King should keep his fist off the throte of liberty. He said yes the Stamp Act was repealed but George had others up his royal sleeve. Mr. Donaughby said he did as the Bible says and gives unto Ceser what belongs to Ceser. It seems to me that King George is like Mr. Whitley, dirty and mean. I *wonder why Mr. Conner is angry about King George but not about Mr. Whitley.*

Tomorrow we take Puddle to River's Pine for shoing. I want to see Gaddi. I havnt seen him for five months. When I see him we can only talk a few minits, but I like it the same, to see what he is doing.

I am ten years old. Mr. Donaughby said seventeen is the proper age for an aprentise to take horses to and fro alone. I know my way on the road. I have lerned to ride. I would be careful. I would take my paper and not speak to anyone because a negro alone is offen thoght of as a runaway slave.

I have new shoes. Mr. Donaughby got them for me for being his aprentise.

I write now in my break from schooling. I was alowed to bring paper and ink outside. Mrs. Donaughby alows me to write some of my thoughts now. I no longer copy only the Bible or from the New Englin Primer. Mrs. Donaughby said I should want for someone for whome to write letters as pratise. But I know nobody who can write to whom I would send a letter. So I keep this jornal.

I wish Gaddi could write. But he is a slave. And a slave could die for lerning to read and write.

8

CALEB PUT THE pen down beside the ink pot, and studied the journal page he had been writing. Mrs. Donaughby said she would check his work when he was done, as he had been late to school this morning for helping with a new gelding, and had missed the penmanship lesson. This paper was fairly tidy and neat, with only slight traces of unevenness from the board on which the paper had been resting. He felt pride in his work. Pride was a sin, but how was he to not feel his penmanship was nicely done, by telling himself it was poor?

The April afternoon was warm, with the scents of hyacinths and daffodils growing along the Donaughby fence. Caleb sat leaning against a dogwood tree heavy with white blossoms. The boys of Mrs. Donaughby's school had been given leave to eat before returning to studies.

Caleb opened the napkin his mother had filled for him, and picked at the biscuit and cheese inside. He wished that when he was through eating, he could run off to other things rather than returning to the shed for cyphering. There was too much going on in the world to be confined to the schoolhouse. There were four new foals in the field who needed halter training. There were fish in the spring-high water of the creek, ready to be hauled up on a hook. In the distance Caleb could see buzzards hovering and diving. There was something dead there, and he was curious to see what it might be. If he ran off, could he blame his wayward feet for taking him astray? Would Mrs. Donaughby fault the feet and not the boy? In a week, school would be done until the fall. What difference could a few more days make?

Beneath a lumpy-trunked oak not far from the dogwood sat the other boys. They were eating and talking as the shadows of the tree branches stroked their pale faces. There were five of them, all white boys, all Quaker boys. They dressed in black trousers and broad Quaker hats. Three were Sanford brothers, and two were Martin brothers. They lived on farms nearby and walked to the Donaughby farm on school days.

"Caleb!" It was Jeremiah Martin, the eldest at thirteen, sitting beneath the tree with his brother and the other boys. He'd finished eating and was now bouncing a pebble up and down in his hand.

"What do you want, Jeremiah?"

"Come over here. I do not mean to shout to be heard."

"I think not."

"I do not mean to make sport of you. Come over."

Caleb stood and carried two uneaten biscuits to the oak tree. He sat down and crossed his legs. He was cautious of Jeremiah, as the boy sometimes called him "paddle-paw."

Jeremiah said, "Has thou heard of the row in Boston?"

Caleb shook his head. "No. What row was that?"

"Mother said we weren't to talk about the fighting," said Jeremiah's nine-year-old brother, Abraham. Caleb liked Abraham. He also liked the Sanford brothers, Gabriel, Michael, and Joshua. They were quiet, thoughtful, and generous. But Jeremiah was another matter.

"Hush, Abraham." Jeremiah lowered his voice and leaned forward. Mrs. Donaughby was inside the shed and it wouldn't do for her to hear this conversation. "A bloody clash it was. I heard about it from my eldest brother, Joseph, who returned home from the north last week. Men were in the streets of Boston the fifth of March, taunting the British soldiers who were attempting to keep the peace."

"Shhh, Jeremiah, thou shouldn't..." began Abraham.

"Thou shant tell thy older brother what to say and what not to say!" growled Jeremiah. Abraham wrapped his arms around his knees and frowned at the ground.

"The British soldiers were forced to fire their muskets into the crowd," continued Jeremiah, "and they killed five in that single moment! Bloody and dead, they were. They would not have been shot if they had not threatened the soldiers, but they did. And I heard one man who got shot was a Negro called Crispus Attucks. What do you think of that, Caleb? A Negro?"

Caleb thought a man being shot was a sad thing.

"Does thou know what I think?" asked Jeremiah.

He grinned a suddenly ugly grin. "I think that Attucks started the disturbance. He could not help himself because Negroes are prone to act without thinking."

Seven-year-old Gabriel Sanford, a small blond boy with light blue eyes, jumped to his feet. "Jeremiah, Satan has hold of thy tongue!"

"Hush, Gabriel, thou art such a child in thy thoughts."

"I shall tell Mrs. Donaughby!"

"Thou shall do no such thing," said Jeremiah. "Telling tales on another is a sin."

"So is speaking ill of another!"

"Do not correct thy elders! Sit and hold thy tongue!"

Gabriel, looking both confused and upset, plopped back down to the grass. He looked at his brothers, both blond and blue-eyed, who scratched at their heads beneath their black hats and said nothing.

"Gabriel is right," said Caleb. "Hush, Jeremiah."

"My brother Joseph is right," said Jeremiah. He pulled at his nose and sniffed. "He has seen a great deal in his travels. He says most Quakers have the wrong idea. He says it is indeed God's will that the white men own the black. Why, our forefather William Penn saw nothing unjust in owning slaves. Negroes are weak and have little minds. Thee may be good with horses but I've a little yellow dog and he is as good at putting a horse at ease as thee."

Caleb felt his blood go cold in his arms. His hands drew up into fists. *No!* he told himself. *Fighting is wrong.* But his hands shook and he felt heat rise in his chest.

"Yes," Jeremiah continued. "In Boston a Negro man got himself and others killed by challenging the British soldiers because he had no thoughts to hold him back. A silly black rebel, like a gnat against a falcon."

"A white man may have started the row," said Caleb.

"No," said Jeremiah. He stretched his arms up over his head. "I think not. Negroes cannot be trusted."

"Why do you say such a thing?" Caleb demanded.

"I think the Negro animal Crispus Attucks . . ."

And then Caleb could hold himself no longer. He lunged forward and slammed his fists into Jeremiah's chest. The boy's breath whooshed from his lungs. He crumpled backward.

"Caleb!" shouted Michael Sanford.

Jeremiah gasped, but in a second he was on his feet, his eyes glaring and his cheeks flushed. "Thou wants to fight with me?"

Caleb jumped up. "Say you are wrong!"

"I am not wrong!" Jeremiah swung a fist at Caleb's jaw. It landed with a crack and a shattering of pain. Caleb swung back, missed, then fell into Jeremiah. The two boys rolled in the grass, pounding each other, kicking, and coughing with each blow. Jeremiah's hat was squashed in the tussle.

The three Sanford boys and Abraham Martin were on their feet now, staring in disbelief.

"See?" Jeremiah panted as Caleb yanked his hair. "Blacks cannot stop themselves from getting into trouble!"

"Say you were wrong!" shouted Caleb.

"No!"

Jeremiah flipped his body, turning Caleb onto his back, and he put his forearm across Caleb's throat. He raised up, putting his weight into the arm and cutting the air from Caleb's lungs. "Thee do not read nor write as well as we do! Thee cannot do addition as well as we. It is proof, Caleb, of thy inferiority. Inferiors need masters!"

Caleb tried to shake his head and buck Jeremiah off but the boy was heavier by a good twenty pounds.

"It's no shame to be what thou are," said Jeremiah. "A mule is a mule, a paddle-paw a paddle-paw! You are a Negro who can be only ignorant. It is best to admit it!"

Caleb clawed at Jeremiah's arm and Jeremiah bit Caleb's hands. Caleb's vision began to shimmer and fade. He felt as if he was going to vomit. He could hear the other Quaker boys standing nearby, crying, "Stop it! Stop it!"

And then the weight was off his throat, and another voice, this one a shrill female voice, was shouting, "Cease this moment! You boys cease now!"

Caleb rolled over onto his stomach, gasping for air. Each breath stung like bramble thorns. He closed his eyes and stars spun on the darkness of his lids.

"Stand!" came Mrs. Donaughby's voice from over his head.

"I can't . . ."

"Get up this moment!"

Caleb drew his knees up under him, and slowly he stood. The whole world was spinning.

Mrs. Donaughby didn't ask what had brought on the fight. It didn't matter. Fighting was a sin, and there was never a reason for violence. God demanded meekness. The Bible said it was the meek who would inherit the earth, not willful boys. She dismissed the younger children to go read their primers in front of the house. Then she took Jeremiah and Caleb back inside the little shed schoolhouse and beat the sinfulness out of them with a lilac switch.

School was dismissed early as Mrs. Donaughby was too upset to teach. She tried, but anger, which was a sin, too, kept welling up in her normally placid face, and not twenty minutes after the fight, she said it was time to stop for the day. The Quaker boys were directed to go immediately home, but Caleb was called to the Donaughby house where his mother was helping with the new baby, Mercy.

"She must know what is in thy heart, Caleb," Mrs. Donaughby said as she took Caleb through the back gate and around the side of the house. Caleb's legs still stung where the switch had bit his skin, but his soul stung more than his legs. Mrs. Donaughby had not allowed Caleb to explain what had happened, and he was certain that if she'd known, she would have been less severe. She would have realized that Jeremiah had been unChristian. Caleb's webbed hand opened and closed nervously inside the fist of the other.

The Donaughby house was not much larger than the hut in which the Jacobsons lived, with the same dark, rough-hewn walls and the stone fireplace. But this home had two rooms and a ladder-accessible loft. The front room, in which Caleb now stood, had a table and chairs, a trunk on which sat a lantern, pegs lining the wall and strewn with family cloaks, a spinning wheel and loom, and a Bible on the mantle above the hearth. Through the door to the second room, two beds and a cradle were visible. Mr. and Mrs. Donaughby slept there with the two youngest girls. The loft was the sleeping place for the other three girls.

Four of the five Quaker girls were seated at the front room table, dressed in identical black dresses and bonnets. The two youngest were carding wool with sharp-toothed combs, removing burrs and smoothing the soft white fibers for weaving. Charity, now eleven, and Patience, now nine, were stitching petticoats. All four glanced at Caleb and then immediately back at their work. Patience rolled her eyes as she put her needle back into the fabric. Clearly she found humor in the fact that Caleb had done something so serious it required the intervention of his mother.

But Charity appeared concerned. Over the past few years, she had become Caleb's friend. They did not speak often, for their lives were quite removed, yet on occasion when Caleb was in the horse field with a colt that needed to be trained to halter and Charity was alone in the vegetable garden, he would call to her and ask how she fared, and she would ask him what new things he had seen on his travels, and would insist he give her details of the sights and sounds beyond the boundaries of Quality and Quantity.

Embarrassed, Caleb looked away from the girl, and made to study the hunting guns on the wall rack.

Mrs. Donaughby went into the back room and Caleb could hear her urgent whispers. A moment later, Francis appeared, wiping her hands on a towel. Her good eye stared at him coolly. Caleb took a step toward the front door. Certainly Francis wouldn't swat him in front of the Donaughbys! She wouldn't humiliate him in such a way!

Patience giggled. Charity shook her sister's arm sternly.

With a sharp turn of her head, Francis indicated that Caleb was to follow her outside. They walked several yards, and stopped by the woodbin.

Francis said, "I'm shamed, Caleb. You have been fighting! What were you thinking?"

Caleb could feel the trembling of her hand on his arm. Fighting was much worse than being late or forgetting to latch the garden gate. But she had to understand. She had to know that he was not totally at fault. "You didn't hear the things Jeremiah said!" Caleb insisted.

"There are no excuses," said Francis. Her good eye was now brimming, and Caleb could see that she was going to cry. She rarely cried, and he hated when she did so, because the cause was always him.

"Mother," he tried to sound like an adult, so she would hear him through her disappointment. "Jeremiah was saying things about Negroes, cruel things, something I'm certain his mother would not want him to . . ."

But Francis held up her hand to silence him. She didn't want to know more. There were no excuses. "You'll go home," she said. "You'll put on the water, and peel the carrots and potatoes. Feed the chickens and clean out the pig's pen. Sweep the floor. Empty the ticks and put in fresh straw. Practice your penmanship without a single mistake, writing of your sorrow at raising a hand against a fellow. I will look for all these things upon my return."

Caleb watched as his mother walked back into the Donaughby house, striding defiantly. He stood for a moment, unable to move. She didn't care that Jeremiah had spoken dreadful lies, and that every other boy had heard him.

He returned to the hut at the edge of the farm and did his chores. The sun was low in the sky behind the forest when he was finished, and he was streaked with grit and pig's slime. He rubbed the filth from his arms and face with a cloth, changed into a clean shirt—the only other one he owned—lit a candle and put it on the table. Standing with his arms crossed, he watched the flames dance on the wicks.

He took a sheet of paper, a pen, and a bottle of ink from a wooden box on a wall shelf. His mother had given him the paper and a pouch of ink-powder at Christmastime, purchased by Mr. Donaughby at the Tavern, to encourage his writing. The pen he had made himself the way Mrs. Donaughby had taught him by shaving and splitting the tip of a sturdy goose feather. The ink he made with the ink-powder, vinegar, and water. The quality was only fair, but no worse than that used by the Quaker boys. Caleb sat at the table, dipped the pen into the ink, and put the tip to the page. He wrote:

Mother wants me to write that I was wrong to fight with Jerimiha. That I'm sorry. But I'm not sory I am angry. She did not want to hear that the boy told lies about black men. She did not want to know it made me angry. It hurts more the way she acted than the way Jerimiha acted.

I shall be glad to go to rivers pine tomorrow with Mr. Donaughby to see the new horse. I shall be glad to not have school and have to tolorate Jerimiha and his sour self.

I wonder if Jerimiha will own slaves some day as Mr. Whitly does. I should not be serprised.

Why doesn't God make every one love each other like Jesus said? Maybe God was daydreaming when he created people's hearts. I get spanked when I daydream. Who would spank God?

9

HE HID THE paper he had just written beneath a stone at the back of the fireplace. It would never do for anyone to read his thoughts. Maybe God wouldn't even find it, back in the shadows.

He got out a second sheet of paper. And, for his mother to see he wrote:

I shall not fight.
The Lord forbbids it.
Love one an other.
I am sorry that I hit Jerimiha.
Forgive me Lord.
Peace be with us.
I am gravely sorry.

❧ 10 ❧

CALEB HELD THE reins of the chestnut mare as Mr. Whitley, in his leather mitts and dirty silk shirt, pulled himself up into the saddle with an audible "umph." This mare was a new horse, one the man bought at a King's Crown Tavern auction, and she was just about as pompous and nasty as the man, himself.

"Watch it there, boy, or I'll have your hide as well as this nag's!" said Mr. Whitley to Caleb as he slipped his feet into the stirrups and collected the reins. "If I'm thrown before I am settled, it shall be on your black head!"

Caleb said nothing, but blew gently on the muzzle of the mare to keep her still. He knew Mr. Whitley's rantings well, for he was fourteen now, and along with his knowledge of horses he had also gained a knowledge of white men, and looked away and never spoke a word unless a direct question was put to him. But as Caleb had accepted how to deal with Mr. Whitley, the Master of River's Pine had reluctantly accepted that Caleb had come to be one of the best horse handlers within fifteen miles. However, it was obvious that the truth sat hard on the fat man. He sent his green horses to Quality and Quantity because he knew he would get back animals quieted to saddle or harness. But it grated the man intensely that a free black was responsible, and he never made to hide his distaste.

"Observe how she moves," said Mr. Whitley. "Like a bloody king, she does, making as if to be in charge of that which she has no business! But she will learn her place!"

Caleb let go and stepped back. In the shade of the barn nearby, Mr. Donaughby stood watching, arms crossed.

The mare shook the reins, and locked her hind legs. Mr. Whitley squeezed his massive thighs against the horse's sides. The mare shook the reins again, and leaned backward.

"Hold there!" said Mr. Whitley. "Don't you dare attempt to be rid of me!" The horse made a deep rumbling sound in her throat, but did not move forward.

Nearby, the slaves of River's Pine were hard at their tasks. At the tanning shack children scraped hides and men soaked them in vats. Deer skins were stretched on frames, soon to be sold or traded with men down at the King's Crown Tavern. A fire roared inside the blacksmith shed, and the sound of ringing metal was sharp on the October air. In the paddocks by the barn, Mr. Whitley's horses watched their newest companion try to outwit the Master. The tobacco barns were nearly empty, with the year's crop having been dried, barrelled, and rolled far away down the road. In the field behind the barn, slaves dotted the barren fields, planting late-season beans.

The chestnut mare jerked the reins through Mr. Whitley's fingers and gained her head. Caleb thought, *She is going to buck,* but he did not say it, because it would mean a crop to his shoulder. In that moment, the horse threw her hind legs out and her back up, and Mr. Whitley was airborne. His tri-cornered hat popped from his head, and his eyes flew wide.

"Halt . . . !" he began, but the word was jammed back into the man's mouth as he struck the ground like a sack of rocks.

The mare trotted to the paddock where the other horses stood, slipped her head over the top fence rail and nipped at the nearest one.

"Damn!" cried Mr. Whitley, pushing himself to his feet. Red, furious blossoms appeared on his cheeks. "Swindled, I was! Good pounds wasted on a demon!"

Out of the corner of his eye, Caleb saw Gaddi come out of the blacksmith shop with a crate full of latches and hinges. The last time Caleb had been to River's Pine, Gaddi told him he had been put to mending and building fences and gates. This job, Gaddi had said, was never-ending, as the plantation had more fences than the sky had stars, and there was always fixing to do.

Gaddi gave Caleb a quick glance over his shoulder and a nearly indistinguishable nod of recognition, then hastened to the wagon up the lane. In the back of the wagon, three other slaves adjusted newly split logs and planks. They were already sweating in the early morning. On a horse beside the wagon sat Grundy, one of Mr. Whitley's four overseers, a man Caleb had come to know at a distance as short, portly, yet frighteningly quick and obedient to his Master. When Grundy took a crew to clear brush or mend roads, he carried with him tools he considered necessary for the control of darkies—a whip and pistol. Gaddi had told Caleb that Grundy had shot a slave in the foot once for spilling a pouch of nails. Grundy had explained to Mr. Whitley that the slave had tried to run away. Grundy had been awarded a flask of whiskey for his good work. The slave had been lame for a month, and then his rotten foot had to be cut off to save the leg.

The wagon rambled off up the lane, and disappeared. Caleb wished to have a moment to speak with his friend, though that was often not possible.

"Get that mule!" cried Mr. Whitley, making to slap Caleb with his crop for not paying attention. "Bring her to me!"

Caleb went to the horse, saying "Ho there, ho," and the horse, with bared teeth and flashing tail, allowed him to touch her neck and pick up the reins, which had tangled and broken beneath the mare's hooves. Caleb whispered into her ear, "You've got yourself bought by the wrong man, horse."

He led her back to Mr. Whitley. Mr. Whitley took one broken rein and jerked it savagely, cutting the horse's mouth with the bit. Caleb cringed.

"I see thy trouble," said Mr. Donaughby, coming out of the shade of the barn, rubbing his beard-covered chin. "A challenge it shall be. But we have success with horses, and I do not see that this shall be any different. We shall keep her several weeks and shall return a new animal."

But Mr. Whitley shook his head. "Not this time."

"I beg your pardon, sir?" asked Mr. Donaughby.

"I should want to be part of this mare's training," said the fat man. "I do not want her taken off the property. She irritates me, and I am bound to make her know it. I want her trained here at River's Pine under my supervision."

"Mr. Whitley," said Mr. Donaughby. "I must return to my home. I have family and business. When thee sent thy servant for us, there was no mention that thee were expecting me to stay. I am sorry. I cannot do it."

"I don't mean you," said Mr. Whitley. "Your blackie can stay. He's got that . . . that *way* with animals." Mr. Whitley brushed his hand in the air, making Caleb's talent seem at once needed and trivial. "I should require him but a week or so. That would not be a problem, would it, sir?"

Caleb's mouth went dry. He looked at Mr. Donaughby, hoping the man would come to his aid. He could not stay here, not for a week, not even for one night.

"Sir?" repeated Mr. Whitley. "You would find your pocket the heavier, as I will pay a stipend for keeping the boy." He paused, then added, "And he shall have lodging and sustenance, of course. I am a fair man."

Mr. Donaughby reached beneath his hat and worked his fingers against his head, scratching thoughtfully, then dropped it to his side. He did not look at Caleb as he answered. "A week it is, then. I shall inform the boy's mother that he has been detained. I will come for . . ."

"I shall send him back at the end of our time," said Mr. Whitley. "I'll have the boy escorted to your farm."

"I give my approval," said Mr. Donaughby. He looked at Caleb, and Caleb could see he wanted no discussion. "Be obedient and humble," he told Caleb. "Do thy duty. I shall see thee in a week's time."

Obedient? To this cruel man? Caleb had to speak. "My mother will worry herself ill," he said, stepping a distance from Mr. Whitley should he decide his words were worth a whack. "Though I am nearly a man she's always in a fret about my where abouts."

"My judgment is sound," said Mr. Donaughby. "Thee are my apprentice and shall do as I say. A week's time." He went to his wagon. Caleb stared as he slapped the reins against Puddle's back and they pulled away, down the lane toward the distant bridge, and at last vanished behind the trees.

Caleb looked back at Mr. Whitley, who was gazing at him with his dark, weasel eyes.

Then the man handed the rein to Caleb and said, "Put the mare in the empty corral. Wait for me."

Caleb swallowed hard. He said, "Yes, sir."

Mr. Whitley watched him for a long moment, as if expecting Caleb to add to his reply "Master Whitley," but then he rubbed his neck, laughed a single, dry laugh, and walked off between the barn and the corral toward the lane that led to the distant house on the hill.

Caleb stared at the mare, suddenly feeling less than fourteen, feeling much like he did when he was six and had come to River's Pine the first time.

"Out the way, boy!"

Caleb glanced over. An old, wrinkled man was pushing a cart full of stones toward him. He jerked his nearly bald head, indicating that Caleb should move. Caleb guessed that if the man stopped, he might not be able to get started again. His arms were bony, his legs withered brown sticks. Caleb urged the mare out of the way. The man continued on, up the lane and over the knoll toward the cabins.

Caleb led the mare to the empty corral and led her inside. In the corral next to them, the other horses trotted around and nickered. Caleb sat on the lowest fence plank, digging his heels into the dirt to keep from slipping off. The mare touched him with his nose. He touched her back, and whispered, "Five days. Six days. That's not so long. I can manage anything for six days." And then he put his hand to his mouth, because once, long ago, Gaddi had told him that Mr. Whitley had hawk ears and could hear anything for miles.

And if he heard, he might just do all he could to give Caleb five days he could not manage.

It was growing dark. The sky had shifted from pale blue to the slate gray of creek bed rocks. A single star poked through the veil of the sky to the west, and crickets began to speak to each other with their mysterious chatterings.

Caleb still sat in the paddock, and Mr. Whitley had not returned. His back had begun to stiffen, so he had plopped down on the ground, knowing the mare would not step on him, that she, like other horses, trusted him and felt safe in his presence. But the hours had crawled by, and he was afraid to leave the paddock in search of something to eat for fear the man would return that very moment.

I'm not a slave, he thought as he watched the mare on the far side of the corral, snuffling the dirt in search of a bit of hay or grain, yet finding nothing. *I'm a free boy! I should not be treated such!*

Beyond the far corral fence, Caleb could see the slaves in the field converging and walking toward the lane, shadows among the shadows. Two men on horseback flanked them as if they were a herd of cattle. They came in a wave, crossing the lane and then walking between the barn and paddock, dressed in old clothes and shawls and scarves, many with rags tied around hands and otherwise bare feet. They spoke quietly to each other as if fearing the wrath of the absent Master Whitley.

The men on horses followed, dismounted near Caleb, then took their horses into the barn. They laughed with each other as they emerged, oblivious to the boy in the paddock. The slaves continued up the lane toward the cottages. Their day, it seemed, was over.

But what about me? Caleb stomped his foot furiously. Dust swirled like gnats. The horse glanced over, then continued to dig at the ground in search of something to eat.

The slaves at the leather shack put up their scraping knives. The blacksmith shop at last went quiet and the glow of the great fireplace within dimmed. The wagon with the fence menders had returned, and the wagon had been put into the barn. Caleb had watched for Gaddi, but had not seen him.

The darkness thickened, and soon Caleb saw a faint glow up the lane where the cabins stood. The moon made its appearance, holding to the sky like a cold sickle.

Caleb clenched his fists. He looked back and forth, wishing someone would come and tell him what he was supposed to do. Mr. Whitley had clearly forgotten, or had intentionally left him alone.

He wants to put me in my place, Caleb thought. *I don't belong to him; he can't do this to me!* The air was cooling with the nighttime. He shivered.

"Boy," came a voice from the darkness. Caleb's head snapped up. He saw the outline of a stout man by the paddock gate. It was Grundy. "Mr. Whitley says he'll train the horse in the morning. To bed with you!"

"Where do I sleep?" The man strolled away, his leather boots creaking.

"Where do I sleep?" called Caleb.

There was no answer.

Caleb found a bucket in the barn, and dipped it in the trough by the leather shack. He placed it in the paddock for the mare, who was already sucking water out of it before he could place it on the ground. The horses in the other paddock had been fed, but not this one. Not for the entire afternoon and evening. Mr. Whitley was trying to teach the mare a lesson as he was trying to teach one to Caleb.

The specter of night hung like a crop over Caleb's head.

He took a deep breath and turned up the lane, then followed the glow of fire and the sound of voices, to the cabins on the far side of the knoll.

11

BOY, YOU LOOK a fright," said the old woman by the fire outside the cabin. She was squatting by a large pot, stirring a paddle in the bubbling depths. Steam rose like ghosts to the blackness above. In the doorway behind her stood three children, gawking at Caleb. Light from the fire fluttered over the woman's face, making her skin appear as bark on an ancient tree crawling with insects.

The cabin was long and flat-roofed, with a single door and a single window. A stone chimney rose from one end. There was a fence about the cabin, made of woven sticks, and a small plot of a garden within. Down the lane were at least another ten cabins, identical to the first, with fires dotting the darkness. People meandered in and out of the doors, doing what Caleb had always thought of as daily chores. Yet these were being done at night. Weeding gardens. Chopping firewood. Washing clothes, churning butter, boiling soap. *Such a life,* Caleb thought, *that day chores must be done after a day full of hard labor and beatings.*

"You that horse boy?" asked the woman.

Caleb nodded.

"What you doing here?"

"I don't know where else to sleep."

"Who you know here?"

"Nobody. Gaddi."

"Gaddi," said the old woman. She lifted the paddle from her pot, bringing with it a thick coating of lard. Two of the little girls from the cabin ran out and leaned against the old woman. They grinned at Caleb. The old woman put the paddle back into the pot. "Gaddi, that young powder keg. He's far 'side, down there with Tall Joe."

"Thank you, ma'am," said Caleb.

"Ah!" The woman laughed. Caleb could see she had exactly one tooth in her head. "I ain't a ma'am, ma'ams is women in hoop skirts and lace gloves."

Caleb moved down the row. A skeletal dog sniffed at Caleb's ankles then stumbled away. Inside cabin doorways, Caleb could see babies and old people in candlelight. Outside in the yards in the firelight, women strained with hoes over potato hills and draped clean, wet clothes over the fence tops. Amid the blouses and trousers were scads of hand and foot rags, dangling from the fence like tiny, stained flags. Several men were stacking wood. One man cut the head from a chicken with a sharpened stick, then handed the dancing carcass to nearby children, who sat on it to pluck the feathers. The slaves looked at Caleb as he passed, and nodded a greeting. Caleb nodded in return.

From the end of the lane, down near a night-shrouded oak tree where a huge bonfire roared, Caleb could hear laughing and cheering. Shadows flashed across the ground. The silhouettes of men ringed the fire, their hands raised in the air, waving wildly. Caleb stopped and squinted, uncertain if he should continue.

"That's Gaddi and Tall Joe," said a young woman in the cabin doorway next to Caleb. "Men idiots, down there bettin'. Got nothing to bet, but there they go!"

"Betting on what?" Caleb turned toward the woman. In the wash of light of the candle she was holding, he could see she was very pretty, perhaps sixteen, with expressive eyes.

"Those fighting cocks," she said sourly. "Idiots. Sound like white men, bettin' on whether the King's soldiers or the colony's militia would win at battle."

Caleb looked back at the gathering. He couldn't hear roosters, only thumps and thuds and cheers.

"They're fighting cocks?" Caleb asked.

"Oh, I guess they are at that!" said the young woman. "You that horse boy?"

Caleb nodded.

"Why you here? You a white Negro, not a black Negro."

"What do you mean?"

She laughed. "Sportin' with you. Go on and see Gaddi and Tall Joe. See how time's wasted when there's none to waste!"

Caleb moved toward the bonfire. Several men noticed him, laughed, and moved aside for him to see. Caleb stared.

"Wan' your turn next, horse boy?" asked one man with a tattered blue shirt and scarred neck. "Winner take you, what'cha say? You thin, but I bet'cha feisty!"

In the center of the ring of spectators, near the

fire, two figures were fighting. Men, not roosters, throwing punches, kicking, wrestling, grunting. They spun around, one locking his foot around the other's ankle and driving him to the ground. Then he was atop him, snarling, trying to grab for both the slashing hands to pin them down.

"Yes'sir!" called the man beside Caleb. "Most over now! Most done! Gonna have it in just a moment!"

"Get up Gaddi!" shouted another man across the opening, his face obscured through the leaping flames of the fire. "Don' make me lose my wager! I'll beat you myself if you do!"

The brawlers were a tall man Caleb didn't know and Gaddi. Gaddi was down, the other man was atop him, blocking blows with his forearms and gasping through clenched teeth. Gaddi had blood streaked on his cheeks, neck, and hair.

"Stop it!" Caleb cried.

Gaddi tried to roll over and throw the other man to the dirt, but the man made a sound in his throat like that of an enraged bull, and snatched Gaddi's hand. He wrenched it up and over Gaddi's head and clawed for the other.

"Ah yes'sir!" shouted some of the men in the circle. Two began to dance, swinging each other by the elbows.

"Stop!" cried Caleb. He dashed into the middle of the circle and fell on the man on Gaddi. "Let him up!"

"What's this now?" demanded a man in the circle. "Boy, get'cher bothersome self out o' there now!"

But Caleb dug his fingers into the back of the tall man, and yanked the handful of shirt as hard as he could, hoping to dislodge the man. The shirt ripped in his grasp, and the man looked over his shoulder at Caleb.

"Get off me, boy!" he shouted.

"Leave him be!" cried Caleb. "I won't see him killed like a rooster, I won't see him with a broken neck! Let him up!"

"Hell and damnation with it all!" said the tall man. He swung himself off Gaddi and jumped to his feet, grabbing Caleb painfully by the upper arm and yanking him upward, too. "You ruined the match!" He shoved Caleb. Caleb stumbled backward toward the fire, his foot going down near the hot blaze. He jumped out of the way, but turned and pointed a threatening finger at the tall man.

"You would've killed Gaddi!" he said. His voice was shaking madly, and his heart slammed like thunder.

The tall man stared at Caleb, his brows drawn upward in confusion and his hands balled into fists. Then, slowly, a ripple of sour laughter burst from his lips, and then men in the circle began to laugh, too. It was a harsh, mean sound.

"Got you a champion, Gaddi," said one. "Need him like a hole in the head, don' cha?"

Gaddi, still on the ground, made an exasperated sound through his teeth. He pushed himself up with effort, brushed himself off, then walked over to where Caleb stood.

"What're you doing?" he demanded.

"Trying to keep you from getting killed!"

"Tall Joe wouldn't kill me," snarled Gaddi. "He'd throw both my hands up over my head if he could, then he'd be the winner. Fight over. But I woulda thrown him off, I was gonna throw him off, and throw his hands up over his head and be the

winner myself. But here you come! Out of nowhere, trying to save something that doesn't need
savin'! Ruinin' it all!"

Caleb didn't know what to say.

Gaddi wiped his face with the back of his hand.
His eyes seemed hazy, and he shook his head as if
to clear his vision. He demanded, "Shouldn't you
be back home with your mama and your Quakers?"

Caleb was too stunned to speak. Gaddi had been
in danger and Caleb had saved him. And yet Gaddi
was furious.

"I have to stay here," Caleb answered.

The men in the circle were beginning to break
away and leave with shakes of their heads. The tall
man said, "That one was mine!," then gave Gaddi
a healthy clout on the shoulder before moving off.

Gaddi said, "Caleb, what you just don't know
. . . !" Then he closed his eyes, shook his head, and
said in a quieter voice, "Go home, Caleb. You're a
free boy, you can go whenever and wherever you
like!"

"Mr. Whitley said I have to stay the week to help
him with his new mare."

"That devil's mare? Ha! She make progress?"

"No," said Caleb. "I sat in the corral for hours.
Mr. Whitley told me to wait for him, but he never
came back."

"You a lucky welp!"

"Lucky?"

"You got left alone. What I wouldn't give for a
day of leftin' alone. No work, no yellin', no whips
cuttin' your hide. No blood boilin' to get away, to
find a river to take you to the sea, never to be
caught."

"It *was* terrible," said Caleb, but suddenly it

didn't seem so terrible in comparison.

"Master Whitley teachin' you a lesson," said Gaddi. "He doesn't like black folks knowin' more than him. He knows you got that way with animals. Makes him mad. He needs your help but he's gonna play with you first."

"That's wrong," said Caleb.

"He makes the rules," said Gaddi matter-of-factly. "Where you sleepin'?"

"Don't know."

"There's room in my cabin," said Gaddi.

They walked to the third cabin up the lane and went to the rain barrel, where Gaddi splashed his face liberally with handfuls of water. Caleb followed suit, and took deep sips through his fingers. Water had never tasted so good.

"I can't believe you're talking about Mr. Whitley in such a way," said Caleb at last. "Don't you think he will hear you, even at his house way up on that hill?"

Gaddi tightened his jaw. "I believed that as a child. But I'm a man now, and I know he is no more than a man, either."

"Are you really going to run away from here?"

Gaddi took Caleb sharply by the arm, spilling the little bit of water he still had cupped in his hands. "Who are you, Caleb? A horse boy, a free boy who knows nothing 'bout my life but what you see when you stop by. You just drift along, in and out, not belongin' to anything, just watchin' other people while you train their horses. Don't talk about what you don't know!"

Those who tended the gardens and who chopped the logs were at last putting their tools in the cabins and retiring for the evening. Caleb followed Gaddi into the cabin, his mind stinging with Gaddi's last observations.

On a bench sat several candles, burning low, and on mattresses on the floors, slaves were at last lying down beneath blankets to sleep. Some spoke to each other in soft tones. Others snored or cursed in the beginnings of sleep.

Gaddi sat down on a mattress near the far wall. Caleb followed suit. "You can have my blanket," Gaddi said. "It ain't so cold."

"I don't need it."

"Suit yourself."

Gaddi lay down. Caleb sat still, his legs crossed, listening to the vague whispers around the cabin, watching the candle flames patter on the ceiling.

Then Gaddi said, "You really thought I was going to die in that fight?"

"Yes," said Caleb.

There was a long silence, then, "I have to fight, Caleb."

"It's wrong. God says so."

"All you know. It's what I have to do. Mr. Whitley stopped fighting cocks in June. He said fightin' Negroes's what makes the pounds these days."

"But why do you do it? Do you really want to make him richer?"

"Best fighters get best rations. More flour, a better shirt, a new pair of shoes. There's three of us Master Whitley fights. Me. Tall Jim. Simpleminded boy named Bog who's younger'en you but big as a horse. We practice at night so we can win at the other farms. Some men here like to bet on who'll win a brawl. I'm good, Caleb. Oh, I'm good! Been to two fights south of here, and I won 'em both."

"Oh."

"Master Whitley gave me a set of pots and a new hoe."

They were silent for several long minutes. Then Gaddi said, "You never seen my house. What'dya think?"

"It's fine."

A laugh in the darkness. "Ain't fine. It's crowded. Hardly no furniture. I ain't got no mama here, she got sold off. No daddy, either, he got hanged for stealing chickens from Mr. Whitley's coop when I was two. Only got a sister now. And you? You got a mother, and a bed, and rifle I bet."

"No bed," said Caleb. "And no daddy, either."

"That's right," said Gaddi. "You told me long time ago your daddy saved a man out a river. Your daddy's a hero."

"He is."

"I've been thinkin' 'bout that. When you born, Caleb?"

"Christmas Day. 1759."

"When you say your daddy drowned?"

"The year before my mama came to Maryland."

Another laugh, this one more like a bark. "You're too old to be so ignorant."

"I'm not ignorant! I can read and write!"

"That man couldn'da been your daddy! Maybe he saved somebody from the river, hell, maybe he saved ten people from the river, maybe he really is a hero but that dead man ain't your daddy."

Caleb's arms flushed. "You know nothing about it, Gaddi."

"I know about babies, and I know it takes nine months for a woman to give birth. Your mama told you a lie."

"My mama doesn't lie!"

"Horses take ten months to foal. Women take

nine. No way that dead man's your daddy, what'cha think about that?"

Caleb couldn't answer. He had never considered dates when it came to his heritage. His father was George, son of the slave Jacob who had lived in Boston. His mother never lied. Lying was a sin, like fighting. Suddenly he felt dizzy.

"You got that horse boy there with you, Gaddi?" came a female voice from above. It was the young woman Caleb had seen outside the last cabin, the one who had called the gamblers idiots. She knelt beside the mattress. She smelled good, like bread. "What we supposed to do with a horse boy?"

"His name's Caleb," said Gaddi from his place on the mattress. "Stayin' the week. Master Whitley picked him special to work with that dreadful new mare he got over at the King's Crown Tavern auction last week."

"Too bad," said the woman. She sat next to Caleb. Caleb scooted himself away several inches. She noticed, and chuckled. "We got us a shy one."

"This is Fern," said Gaddi. "Fern, that's Caleb."

"Caleb," said Fern. "You ain't half a bad lookin' boy. Year or two more on you and you'll have women swoonin' and beggin' to jump the broom." She reached out and took his hand. "You just do as you're told here, and—"

Her voice froze, and her hand suddenly jerked free of his. "What's the matter with your hand?" she asked.

Caleb looked down at his hand. It was hard to see in the dim candlelight, but obviously Fern had felt the deformity.

"Nothing," said Caleb hesitantly.

"You got them webbed fingers on your hand," Fern said.

"Well, I . . ."

"God," she said, and the loathing in her voice was worse than any teasing Jeremiah had ever done. "Look at you, you little devil! I can't believe you are staying here, in our very quarters!" She stood and left the cabin in haste, stepping over the sleeping forms as she went.

Caleb watched after her. Then, to Gaddi, he said, "Why did she act so? My hand's not such a dreadful thing."

"I don't know," said Gaddi. "I can't figure women's heads. Go to sleep. Morning comes afore sunup."

Sleep was a long time in coming for Caleb, but the morning wasn't, and before he knew it he was back in the paddock with the orange rays of sunlight piercing the forest to the east, waiting for Mr. Whitley to come and help him with the mare.

❧ 12 ❧

October 25, 1774

I earned four pounds for Mr. Donaughby last week
at River's Pine. The chestnut mare calmed to me and
thus to Mr. Whitley of a sort. At the end of the week
Mr. Whitley sent me home with coins for the Quaker
and not but a weary mind and body for myself. I slept
in Gaddi's cabin those six nights and ate his food.
Fern avoded me as if I had a plage. I kept thinking
about Gaddi's words, that I belong nowhere. I felt
lonely and outcast, indeed, and slept poorly.

Mr. Whitley made sport of me the whole of the six
days, leaving me for hours in the paddock waiting,
and oftentimes striking me if he felt so moved. If I had
my choice, I would never work at River's Pine again,
even if Mr. Whitley were to promise me a field full of
horses and Mr. Donaughby a sack full of silver.

Grundy was ordered to take me home after my long
week at River's Pine. He took me in a wagon down the
rolling road. I said nothing to him for the duration of
the trip for fear of his gun or whip. We reached Kings

Crown Tavern and he stopped for an ale, ordering me to stay outside and wait. He was quite a long while and I took to playing with a mouse I found in the hay of the wagon bed. Then I climbed out to read the broadsides nailed to the tavern. I had seen such notices before, reading the new ones on the many ocasions Mr. Donaughby stops for business at the tavern. Today there were notices ofering rewards for the return of runaway slaves. There were also many notices of anger aganst the newest of King George's acts. The authir of these notices called these acts "Intolerable." He said the colonists were treated like slaves by their king, who closed Boston harbor to comerse, and increased British athority in Masachusets as punishment for loss of tea. He also wrote that there was a meeting of a continental congress in Philadephia last month where the men decided the colonies should no longer import goods from Britan. I laughed sourly at this, for this man writes as though opresion is heaped on white colonists heads only!

A man called to me suddenly. Ho, there, he said. I ran back to the wagon, fearing it was Grundy and he was going to shoot me. But it was a man on a fine gray mount, wearing gray Quaker clothes. I thought I had seen this man before, years back, but he was like a dream that I had nearly forgotten. His skin was black.

The man dismounted and came over to the wagon. He said, Are thee not Adam Donaughby's young friend?

I told him I was the apprentice who lived on the Donaughby farm, and he said he recalled me from year's ago, when I had been a skinny child tending two wild yearlings. Such a memory he had. His name was Benjamin Banneker. He stood with me a long while and we talked.

Mr. Banneker told me that he had met Mr.

*Donaughby some seventeen years earlier when he lived
east up the road. They had attended the same Friends
meetings, before Adam had married and moved deeper
into Maryland's western wilderness. Mr. Banneker said
he lived some fifteen miles east of the tavern, near the
Ellicott Mills, yet on occasion he would come to the
tavern to meet with friends whom he had not seen in a
long while. I asked him why he stayed outside to talk to
me instead of going inside to meet his friends. He said
he was black and though free, not entirely so, for he
was not allowed in the tavern. When his friends
arrived, they would talk and visit in the lean-tos.*

*Then he said to me I saw you looking at the notices
on the wall. Do you read and write? I said yes. He
asked if I had books or papers to read at Quality and
Quantity. I said Mrs. Donaughby has lent me the
Bible, Pilgrim's Progress, Divine Emblems, and Little
Book for Little Children which tells the tales of
Christian martyrs and their tortures. He said he knew
the books. He pulled out of his knapsack several
newspapers, the Maryland Gazette, and said if I would
like I could have them and learn tales of colonies and
their own peculiar tortures. I put them in my shirt for
although Quakers do not generally disapprove of
reading such things, Mr. Donaughby did so forbid it.
He wanted his family to read of God but not so very
much of man.*

*Mr. Banneker asked of my aspirations. I said I
should like to continue training horses. The man
nodded, but then said, whatever you do, son, know
that you have a responsibility and opportunity for
much good, for both man and beast. Take that
responsibility seriously he said, for you never know
when you shall be called to serve.*

*Men came out of the tavern then, several I did not
know and the overseer Grundy. Two enjoined Mr.*

Banneker and they strolled to the lean-tos. Grundy was full of spirits and unsteady on his feet, and he commanded me out of the wagon. How far do ye say is your home he asked. I looked at the ground and said five miles, sir. He said five miles never took the flesh off a blackie's feet, and he would not carry me the rest of the way. He slapped the reins and the wagon was off, returning east from whence it came.

I was alone on foot and night was coming. I had Mama's free paper in my shirt with the Gazettes. But never have I had cause to think much about it. Yet that night I was sore afraid. I walked westward, cursing Grundy and Mr. Whitley. The moon was out allowing me to see my feet in front of me.

Not long hence there came hoof beats and men's voices. I thought of jumping into the brush but if they heard me doing so and caught me they would think for certain I was a slave, run away, and whip me. I continued to walk ahead on the road. My entire body was hot with dread.

One called to me saying black boy where you going? I stopped and looked down and said home to Quality and Quantity sir. He said home to the Lord he guessed as I would be beat to death once they roped me up and returned me to my master. I took out the free paper from my shirt and held it out as the two pulled up next to me, making to knock me over by moving their horses back and forth into me. One scoffed, saying I could have had this forged. But the other said no he knew Mr. Donaughby at Quality and Quantity and that a couple free Negroes lived there. The two spit at me, clouted me on the ear, then laughed and rode into the darkness.

I arrived home well after midnight filthy, shaking with anger and cold and wishing that my shoes were a horse and the paper hiding in my shirt was a sidearm.

13

"WHAT AILS YOU, Caleb?" asked Francis as the two of them stood outside the cabin patching holes in the sides with hot pitch from a dented bucket. Francis had awakened Caleb early and sent him outside in the frost to start a fire beneath the pot full of pitch. Each year the cabin walls would expand and contract with the weather, making gaps between the logs. The cracks needed to be sealed before the threat of snow came upon them in December.

But when his mother spoke to him, Caleb realized he'd been standing with the trowel in his hand long enough for the pitch he'd scooped to cool to a crust.

"You been acting strange since you went to that plantation," said Francis. "You sick?"

Caleb shook his head, although that wasn't wholly the truth. Ever since his week at River's Pine, his learning of the lie his mother had told concerning his father, his walk home, and reading the newspapers Mr. Banneker had given him,

Caleb had been filled with a restlessness that wouldn't subside. He had a hard time concentrating on even the simplest of tasks. He was no longer in school—at fourteen he'd had all the schooling he needed—and so it was not a matter of not keeping up with lessons. But his thoughts wandered when feeding the hogs, lighting the fire, shooting squirrels, or bridling a yearling colt. He would find his thoughts straying to one of the many images that tangled in his soul—slaves fighting each other to earn pots and pans, a man who was not his father saving a drowning man in the river, Fern recoiling at the touch of his hand, white men on horses believing he was a runaway, the story of the burning of a ship in the Annapolis Harbor. These thoughts blurred his concentration.

The *Maryland Gazette* had been hidden in the eaves of the chicken coop, where Caleb would take them out to read when he had a private moment. They contained various articles on various matters from new silversmith shop openings to the Intolerable Acts; yet, Caleb had been fascinated with them all, with each vivid eye witness account to events in Baltimore, Chestertown, and in the capital of Annapolis where the ships were anchored in the waters of the mysterious Chesapeake Bay.

But one story had etched itself deep into Caleb's heart. It read in part:

"The eve of October 19th rang with cries for liberty and freedom on the wharf of our faire capital of Annapolis. Following the example of Boston, where a gathering of the Sons of Liberty on December 16, 1773 did lead protest against British tyranny by dumping 340 chests of tea into the Boston Harbor, Marylanders likewise showed their contempt of the Tea Act by which British Parliament

her and working to catch her breath. "Thank you, son. This animal could have hurt any of us! You, Mr. or Mrs. Donaughby, little Mercy. You stopped it. God bless you, boy."

Caleb dropped the axe to the ground. He looked at the dead fox. It seemed small now, its little black legs curled, its tail limp. A moment ago, he could have sworn it was much bigger. Then Caleb knelt beside his mother.

"Mama, are you hurt?"

"Not much. A scratch from falling."

"Are you certain?"

Francis put out her hand and Caleb helped her up. Then he stared at the dead fox. "We can't let it lie about," he said. "It's as dangerous dead as alive. We must burn it."

Francis nodded. Caleb tore off his hand rags to make a torch. He wrapped them about a small log and lit it with the fire on the hearth.

Back outside, Francis had dragged the dead fox to a spot of bare earth, and was placing twigs and tinder from the log pile around it. Caleb touched the twigs with the burning torch and waited until the sticks smoldered then caught fire. Francis and Caleb watched the scene, until at last the fox's fur began to smoke and smolder, and then was ablaze.

At long last Caleb said, "You were bit, weren't you?"

"Not so bad," said Francis.

"Let me see."

Francis lifted her black skirt several inches. There on her leg was a raw, red gash, smeared in blood. Caleb's blood froze. She had been bitten, and severely. "Mama . . . ," he began.

And then the realization came into his mother's eyes, and several tears dripped down her cheeks, streaking the dust that was there. "I guess it's done, then," she said simply.

The next twenty days were hell. Francis talked of going into the forest and dying there, as she'd heard a slave had done when she was a child back in New York, to save those she loved from the agony of her death. But Mrs. Donaughby would have none of it. Though it was not safe to let Francis stay in the Jacobson hut or the Donaughby farmhouse, the Quaker woman made a tolerable abode from the schoolhouse shed, and tended her dutifully and without emotion. Caleb tried his best to keep his thoughts on his work with Mr. Donaughby, and on feeding the hogs and chickens and cleaning the hut. But late at night he would go to the shed and talk to his mother through the latched window.

For the first few days she was not sick, and Caleb hoped that the fox they had killed did not have the madness after all. But then Francis began to complain of numbness where she had been bitten, and soon afterwards she had a hard time sleeping as her head ached constantly.

Charity Donaughby helped tend Francis, and many evenings when she came out with a bowl of water and rag to ease the fever of Francis's leg, she would pause to speak with Caleb.

"She is in God's hands," Charity said one dark night, as she stood outside the door to the shed and Caleb stood with his arms crossed, leaning against the shed wall, listening to his mother's labored breathing. "We've used all we know to use, herbs, rubs, teas. She can no longer drink for she can barely swallow. There is nothing more to do but ease what we can ease. Pray God she goes easy, and soon."

"It is my fault," said Caleb, looking into Charity's soft blue eyes. "She is dying because of me. I had been thinking grand thoughts, and paying no attention to what was about me. If I'd seen the fox but a minute earlier, I could have had the rifle, and could have still had my mother."

"Caleb, do not blame thyself," said Charity. "God's ways are mysterious, and—"

"No! It is my fault. Vanity, such a sin it is, and it has brought about my mother's death! Imagining myself doing grand things, saving people from oppression, chasing off evil with a wave of my hand! And this is what it has brought me. This is what it has brought my mother."

Charity stood silently for a moment, then said, "God bless thee, Caleb, and bring thee peace." She went into the shed to wash Francis.

It was November 15th when Francis lost consciousness, and November 19th when she died. The service was a simple meeting in the farmhouse, where Mr. Donaughby, Mrs. Donaughby, Charity, and at long last Caleb, spoke up on the matter of Francis Jacobson's life and her eternal rest now with her Lord and Savior. Francis was buried behind the Donaughby garden, where baby Prudence had lain these past eight years.

After the burial, Mr. Donaughby drew Caleb aside and said, "Thee are welcome to stay and continue working as thee has been doing, tending thy plot and training my horses."

Caleb thanked the man. Then he returned to the silent, dark hut on the other side of the cattle field, and pulled up every raspberry bush in a rage with his hands, cutting his palms deeply with the autumn-brittle thorns. Afterward, he sat on his mother's bed and cried, and then found paper and ink, and composed a statement. A vow.

❧ 14 ❧

November 19ʰ, 1774

*My carelessness has brought about the death of my
mother. I have let it happen, God forgive me! I have
never felt such agony, and wonder if I will ever be
happy again.*

*I swear this to be true, before myself and before the
Almighty Lord, that from this day forward I will
humble myself to my duties in life. I shall follow God's
commandments. I shall not be consumed with vane
thoughts nor thoughts of revenge. I shall not find fault
with others. I shall not hate. I shall not be taken with
vain imaginings which, by taking my thoughts from
the present, caused my mother's death.*

I shall shun violence!

*The peace of God be with the spirit of my dear
mother.*

Amen.

Amen.

15

THE MID-APRIL SNOW that had fallen had ended, leaving the rolling ridges of Quality and Quantity shrouded in a thin layer of white. Trees lining the edge of the fields were barren and black, and the horses, digging in the snow with their hooves in search of grass, were just beginning to lose patches of their winter coats.

Caleb held tightly to the long rope in the middle of the white-shrouded field, clucking to the golden mare he called Nosey, urging her to pick up a trot. The horse snorted, shook her mane, and obeyed, lifting her legs high and punching holes in the snow with her well-trimmed hooves.

"Ho there," said Caleb. "Even pace now." He did not need a whip to get her to move. His tone was enough.

The horse slowed, gathered herself, and her circling trot became smooth and graceful.

"Fine," said Caleb approvingly. "Fine, girl."

On Caleb's head was a wool hat Charity Donaughby had knitted him. He also wore a tattered wool jacket and pair of boots Mr. Donaughby had given him several years back. Both the jacket and boots had belonged to Mr. Donaughby when he was a youth, but they were too small for Caleb now. It was 1776 and Caleb was sixteen. The jacket and boots had fit him at fourteen, but now he could barely move his shoulders and toes in them. Two years ago, the Donaughbys had been generous in sharing clothes. But now, with local boycotts on English fabrics and other items, there was less to go around. Less to share. Mrs. Donaughby, a frugal, practical woman, had learned to be even more so, and her daughters' dresses and husbands' shirts lasted well beyond expected.

Though the spring snow was a surprise and inconvenience, it didn't stop anyone on the farm from being about their business. In the barn, Mr. Donaughby was loading the sled with hay to drag out to the field. All eleven horses in Mr. Donaughby's herd had been confined in the barn because of the weather and needed to be out to exercise. But with snow on the ground they would need the hay. As soon as Caleb was finished lunging Nosey, he would take her to the paddock, scrape the sweat from her hide and brush her soundly. A buyer was coming that morning with five pounds, only a fair price for the mare. But everything was tighter now, even the market value for horses.

Outside the Donaughbys' farmhouse, Mrs. Donaughby and her six girls padded about in cloaks and mittens, hanging clothes to dry. Caleb looked in Charity's direction and she looked in his. They exchanged a nod and a smile.

For a half-hour Caleb moved Nosey through her paces. Then he drew her up and gave her a healthy pat on her neck. "I wish I had five pounds myself," he said. "You'd be mine!"

Caleb pulled an apple from his jacket pocket. It was sad looking, found in the bottom of the barrel Caleb had filled the previous autumn. Fresh produce in early spring was rare; only potatoes and apples could keep from rotting, although they often got insects or went soft. He put it in front of Nosey's muzzle, and in an instant she drew it into her lips and was crunching it to bits. Juice oozed from her mouth.

Suddenly, there was the sound of gunfire from the woods beyond the field. Startled, the horses cantered off, sending snow in a spray. Nosey yanked her rope but Caleb held her tightly. "Easy, girl," he said. A few moments later another shot could be heard, then loud laughter.

Caleb squinted. He thought he saw movement in the trees. Perhaps these were hunters, although they sounded much like the men who came in and out of the King's Crown Tavern—drunk. Mr. Donaughby had fencing around his entire property, so if these men were full of spirits, at least they would have to make a wide berth to get to where they were going.

There was another loud laugh and then a man on a gray horse came crashing over the fence. They landed with a thud in the snow of the field, and the man waved his musket in the air over his head. "Liberty!" he cried. "Liberty for Maryland!" Two other men on horseback joined him, hurdling Mr. Donaughby's fence as if it were a fallen log or stream, not the boundary marker of a private farm. One man was astride a white horse, the other on a bay. All three horses were covered with sweat and mud. Side by side now, each with a musket in hand, they trotted toward Caleb.

Mr. Donaughby would order them out, Caleb told himself. *He would tell them they'd made a mistake jumping the fence!*

As the men came closer, Caleb could see that they were not men but boys closer to his own age. Sixteen, perhaps, seventeen. They wore long cloaks, knit scarves, and tall leather boots. On their shoulder straps they carried powder horns and on their belts tomahawks. Tied to their saddles were bulging knapsacks.

Caleb looked toward the barn. Mr. Donaughby was outside now, hitching the hay sled to Puddle. If these rowdy boys stirred up Mr. Donaughby's horses, Caleb would kick himself for doing nothing. Already, he could feel anger creeping up from his gut. He tried to swallow the anger back, but it was persistent, like bees escaping a hive.

I have vowed not to fight, he thought. *But I haven't promised to let a wrong go unchallenged.*

He raised his hand and said in a loud voice, "Leave! You're trespassing!"

The boys drew their horses up just several yards from Caleb. They leaned forward and stared as if they had seen a talking mule. The boy on the bay laughed, an incredulous, evil laugh that reminded Caleb of Mr. Whitley. Then he said, "Did you speak to us, crow?"

Nosey tugged on her lead. Mr. Donaughby's other horses stood in the distance, ears erect, watching. The boy on the white horse rubbed the barrel of his musket along the length of his boot. "And I cannot believe what I am seeing, but are you *looking* at us, slave?"

Fear joined the anger in Caleb's throat. His jaw tightened. His gaze fell to the ground out of habit, but then he made himself look up again. "This land belongs to Mr. Adam Donaughby. It would be best, sirs, if you went back as you came, and go around the property line to the road."

"Friends!" cried the boy on the gray. He seemed to be the most inebriated of the three. He swayed in his saddle. "Will you hear this? A slave telling future soldiers of George Washington where they cannot go? Can we tolerate it?"

The boy on the white horse said, "We cannot have it!"

"We cannot, indeed!" said the boy on the bay.

Nosey tossed her head again and reared. Caleb held on to the lead but did not look away from the boys with their muskets. He repeated, "This is Adam Donaughby's farm. You are here without permission."

The boy on the gray raised his musket and looked down the barrel at Caleb. "The devil you say! We are off to join George Washington in New England to fight the British who deem to steal our liberty and land! No piece of chattel will tell us where to go! I've got this powder-loaded and ready. Stand aside or I'll send your head flying from your neck!"

"Robert, do not shoot him!" said the boy on the bay. "Save your shot for the British!"

"Stand aside," said Robert.

In spite of the cold, Caleb flushed. Everything he'd learned said it was best to hang his head, mutter an apology, and let them go. His declaration from two years back had sworn himself to peace-making. But the hairs on his head, the flesh on his bones would not be calmed.

In a voice he fought to steady Caleb said, "You must leave Mr. Donaughby's property."

With a bellow, Robert raised up in his stirrups and swung his musket at Caleb's head. Caleb jumped out of the way, and the musket barrel cracked his arm instead. Caleb stumbled but kept his balance. Robert urged his mount forward several steps, then swung the musket again. Ducking quickly, Caleb heard the whistle of the air as the musket nearly connected with his ear. Nosey reared again.

"Enough, Robert!" said the boy on the white.

"If we can't subdue a simple field slave, can we deter the British?" demanded Robert. "I say nay!"

"Enough!" said the boy on the bay. "Leave this boy to his work and we shall get on with ours. We do not want to be worn out before we even enlist!"

But Robert swung his musket again. This time Caleb did not jump away but grabbed the weapon with his free hand.

"Let go, slave!"

His whole body shaking, Caleb said, "You are trespassing on Adam Donaughby's land!"

"Let go, slave!"

"Leave this land, sir."

"Let go!" Robert jerked the musket. Caleb jerked back. The boy toppled over the head of his horse and landed on his back. The musket came free in Caleb's grasp.

"He's going to shoot us!" coughed Robert from the ground. In that moment, the other two boys raised their muskets and trained them on Caleb. "These are also powder-ready!" said the boy on the white.

Caleb knew what would happen next. A slave with a gun was subject to being killed on the spot, no questions asked. Gaddi had told him so. *But I'm not a slave!*

Caleb hurled the musket as far as he could from himself. But it wasn't soon enough.

"Get down on your knees," said the boy on the bay. "And pray to God. You have but a few seconds before you meet Him face to face."

"Stop!" The shout came from the far side of the field. Caleb did not turn to see; he kept his eyes on the dark, hollow eyes of the two muskets pointing at his skull. "Stop now! I demand thee to put down thy weapons!"

The muskets aimed at Caleb began to waver.

"Who is that?" asked one.

"I do not know," said the other.

"The master of this farm!" said Robert, standing up and grabbing his horse's reins. "We must get off the land."

"The slave meant to kill us!"

"Do you want to discuss it with him? Do you want to be detained to explain the truth? Or would you rather be on the way to enlist in Washington's army?" Robert jammed his foot in the stirrup and swung himself into his saddle.

The muskets were lowered, and the three boys dug their heels into the horses' sides. With a whoop, they galloped across the snowy field to the northern fence. In unison the horses leapt the fence and they vanished into the forest.

Caleb's knees went instantly weak. His eyes closed.

"Caleb!" Mr. Donaughby's voice was close now, and Caleb opened his eyes. The Quaker man was running as best he could through the snow, his arms out like raven's wings and the brim of his black hat flopping.

"I'm unharmed, sir," said Caleb, opening his eyes.

Mr. Donaughby reached Caleb, then bent over to grasp his knees and his breath. The man rarely ran, and his body was unhappy with the requirement. Then Mr. Donaughby asked "What was going on with those boys?"

"They trespassed. I demanded they leave your pasture."

"And thee fought them?"

Caleb hesitated. He said, "Not quite. They didn't like me correcting them, and came at me. I only defended myself."

Mr. Donaughby frowned, and then rubbed his neck. "I shall defend my own land. I shall not have thee telling anyone who or who should not lay foot here. Do I make myself clear?"

Caleb nodded. "Yes, sir," he said.

"Decisions such as that are mine to make, not thine. No more of this, boy. No more."

"No, sir," said Caleb. The anger had left his stomach, but disappointment and humiliation took its place. No, Caleb did not own this land. He owned not an acre, not a rock. He did not even own the little hut in which he lived, nor the mattress on which he slept. He owned only pots and pans, the clothes on his back, the hat on his head, a few coins he'd been given by Mr. Donaughby for chokecherries or pigs.

In truth, he owned nothing of consequence.

Caleb felt suddenly less than an apprentice. He felt less than a servant.

He felt more like a slave.

Caleb took Nosey to the barn, where the gentleman from a farm to the south had come to take her with him. The man was young and abrupt, dressed like a dandy in silk stockings, and a feathered cap. He thanked Mr. Donaughby for the fine work with the gelding, gave Caleb not even a glance, which was no more than Caleb expected, and rode off on his bay mare leading the new purchase. Caleb stayed to muck out the empty stalls while Mr. Donaughby took his pocketful of earnings to his farmhouse.

The chastisement the Quaker had given Caleb had been no more severe than any in the past, as when Caleb had broken a halter or had spilled a bucket of grain. Yet, this one cut his heart. For even when he had worked beyond his apprenticeship at eighteen, he would still own no land and no hut. He would still look at the ground when white men spoke to him, and still be stopped on the road as a runaway.

He returned to his hut in late afternoon, after working the majority of the day in the barn, cleaning up after the horses that had been confined inside, tossing out soiled straw and putting down clean. He stoked the fire, kicked off his muddy boots, and hung his hat and jacket on a wall peg. He removed his shirt, wet with sweat, and lay it over the chair near the fire to dry.

There was a knock on the hut's door.

Caleb frowned, imagining it was Mr. Donaughby again, with more to add to his previous reprimand. He took a deep breath to still his heart and his tongue, and yanked the door open.

It was Charity, bundled in cloak and bonnet and mittens. Her buttoned-up boots were caked with melting snow. In her hands was a basket draped in a linen napkin. "May I come in?" she asked.

Caleb snatched his wet shirt from the chair and slipped it on. He noticed that his hut had not been swept that day, and that his blanket was in a heap on the bed.

"May I come in?" repeated Charity. "Just for a moment. I'll not stay. I do not mean to burden thee with time."

"Of course," said Caleb. He felt his ears go warm. He didn't want Charity to think he was not a gentleman.

She stepped through the threshold, but came no farther. She held out the basket. "Mother sent this to thee. It's bread. She would have brought it herself but she is nearing her time of delivery. The walk might have been too much."

"Yes, well," said Caleb. Mrs. Donaughby was expecting again. Mr. Donaughby was praying for a boy, but Caleb couldn't imagine the Donaughbys having anything but a crop of girls in black dresses and bonnets.

Caleb put it on the table. He turned back to Charity, who stood still, a gentle smile on her face, curls of blonde hair at her neck beneath her bonnet strings. Caleb felt once more that she and Gaddi were his only friends, yet Gaddi was a slave and she was white. He didn't fit into either's world. It stung his heart.

Then Charity said, "I saw thee in the field with those ruffians. One came at thee, and I so feared for thy safety." She looked at the floor, and a shiver crossed her shoulders. "I thought they were going to harm thee, and although my father was angry that thou challenged them, I was glad to see it. God forgive me, but I was."

"I'm not hurt," said Caleb. He looked at Charity, and wished there was something to do to ease the torment in her eyes. "Thank you for your kindness."

Charity wiped her eyes and said nothing.

"Is there something else?"

Charity nodded slowly. "I wanted to tell thee. Father would have me married in a fortnight. To move to Philadelphia and begin my own family. He says I am well old enough, and shall be a good wife."

"Married?" said Caleb. Certainly Charity, at seventeen, was old enough to become a wife. But the thought was a disturbing surprise, as he couldn't imagine losing her from this farm. The place would be hollow with her gone.

"Who are you to marry?" he asked.

"Jeremiah Martin." This was spoken in nearly a whisper, and in that whisper Caleb could hear that she thought no more of Jeremiah than he did. "I cannot imagine being his wife, Caleb."

"Why would you marry him, then? I don't think your father would force your hand."

"Not so much force," said Charity. "But he has made me know it is my obligation. We have so many mouths to feed, with another any day now. How can I not accept a proposal from a young man who has secured a position and a house?"

"I don't know," said Caleb.

Charity began to cry then. Caleb looked at her for a moment, but then compassion pulled him forward and he took her in his arms. She did not move away, but moved into him, laying her cheek on his shoulder and clutching one of his arms with her small fingers. Caleb suddenly felt tears in his own eyes, and tears in his own soul, knowing that, like his mother, Charity would soon be gone, never to be seen again. He reached up to touch her face, and she turned her face from his shoulder to look at him.

"Charity," he said. And then he kissed her. He had never kissed a girl, and had never known but in his late-night imaginings what it would be like, but now he was, and it was a warm and beautiful thing. She sighed, and her breath on his mouth was sweet. He wrapped his arms around her back, drawing her into him. What if he offered to marry her? The thought was instantly lovely and sad. It would never happen. Could never happen. She was a Quaker girl and he was—

"Charity!" The shout was loud and furious, and immediately Caleb and Charity fell apart to stare at Mr. Donaughby standing in the doorway of Caleb's hut. The man had never looked so angry, and beneath the simple black coat and simple black vest, his body was shaking dreadfully. The basket of jam he'd been holding crashed to the floor, sending shards of pottery and sticky sweetness over the wooden planks. "What are thee doing, daughter? Sweet God in heaven, what are thee about?"

Charity seemed to shrink, pulling her hands to her eyes and covering them as if fearing the fury on her father's face. Caleb stood agape, knowing there was nothing to be said or done, that his actions had sealed whatever consequences were to come.

Mr. Donaughby's usually stoic eyes flashed. "Thy mother sent me with jam for the boy's bread, something she had forgotten to give thee to bring, and I find thee with the boy in a most ungodly fashion? Get thee home! Now!"

Charity rushed from the hut, weeping, and down the snowy path across the cattle field. Caleb was left standing with the shattered jam jugs and the furious father.

Mr. Donaughby said nothing for a very long minute. Caleb remembered when he was six and had feared that the Quaker's silence meant he was in trouble for trying to help a colt from a trap of honey locust thorns. He had found out that the man wasn't angry, only amazed. But this time he knew he was in trouble. There was no mistaking it.

Caleb crossed his arms and waited for the pronouncement.

And it came, with fewer words than he would have thought.

"Thee are to leave by morning," said Mr. Donaughby. "Pack what thee can in a sack, and be gone before I must lay eyes on thee again."

Then the man was gone, out the door, following his daughter back to the log farmhouse.

And Caleb never saw the Quaker nor his daughter again.

❧ 16 ❧

HE HAD TO find a place to live and a means of earning his keep, at least until he could clear his head to make longer-ranged plans. And so it was with dread and resignation that he found himself trudging across the bridge to River's Pine with his sack of pans, clothes, tools, pens, and hunting rifle, ready to ask Mr. Whitley if he might be employed as a horse handler for board and a small fee. Although other farmers in the area knew of his talents, men whose homes he would have preferred, those men were of limited means, and could perhaps have given him board only and no pay. Caleb needed pay. The only option was the fat man's farm.

The trip on the road was uneventful but miserable, as the day was rainy and cold and most travelers had found shelter somewhere until the rain was past. He had the freeman's paper in his shirt, ready should a man on horseback ask for proof of his right to walk the slush-covered road without a master. But for the whole of the thirteen miles he saw no one but a few outside the doorway of the roadside tavern, which had recently been renamed "The Coiled Snake Tavern." The wooden sign with the painting of the king's crown had been smashed with hatchets, and lay in a heap beside the door for all to see. It took Caleb eight hours to reach his destination, and his bones felt every moment of the hike.

As he made his way through the melting cover of snow along the left lane toward the blacksmith shop and tobacco barns of River's Pine, he thought, *I will be all right. I will not have to stay here forever. Earn a few coins and then move again. To a city, perhaps. I have always wanted to see Annapolis. Perhaps even Philadelphia. I do not have to stay here. I'm a free man. I'm a free man.*

Within the depths of the blacksmith shop, the eternal blaze roared. The ping of metal on metal cut the air. Caleb glanced in at the leather aproned men and raised his hand to them. They nodded but kept up their work, leaning over the anvil and into the bellows, creating endless items of metal for their master. No matter if the master even needed them all, they would make them until their dying day. Caleb believed that if these slaves sinned enough to go to hell, their hell would be making latches for Satin for eternity.

Caleb walked on toward the barn. He would stow his sack there, and then seek out Mr. Whitley in order to put his proposal before the man. He hoped the man would say yes, and he feared the man would say yes.

Slaves were in the distant field this evening as the twilight settled on the land, working up the muddy, snowy soil for the spring planting. It would have to be twice as hard to work against the sodden earth, and would have been easier and faster labor to wait a few days for the ground to dry out a bit. But what did a master care that his slaves needed to struggle twice as hard, as long as the chore was done when he wanted it done?

Caleb wondered if Gaddi was out mending fences, or chopping trees. It had been almost a year since he'd seen his friend. That visit had come when one of Mr. Whitley's mares had gone into distress while foaling. Grundy had been sent to bring Caleb to the plantation. The mare had given birth at last, and both horses had survived.

I wonder if Gaddi has room in his cabin for a stray man with little to his name now but a sack of tools and a bit of ink powder? Caleb thought.

He tugged open one side of the barn door and walked in.

It took a few moments for his eyes to adjust. He knew this barn well now, where the tack room was, the feed stall, the bin with the rakes and forks. He could find his way around by feel, smell, and memory. There were three horses in the barn now; he could sense them, could hear their muffled snuffling and stomping in their dense beds of straw. He heard a barn cat stalking a mouse, then felt the rush of tiny feet as the mouse scurried across the toe of his shoe, followed by the cat. They ran into the far recesses of a stall, deeper still, until Caleb could no longer hear them.

But then he heard the heavy breathing. It was near the back of the barn, in a stall to the far left. Caleb knew immediately it was not a horse's breath, but that of a man. Horses did not try to hide their pain from their fellow creatures, but grunted and groaned with fervor. Men, on the other hand, were likely to keep their pain secret.

There was a man in the far stall, and he was hurting.

Caleb left his sack by the door and crept down the center aisle, listening to the breathing. Horses in the stalls stuck their heads out to nuzzle him, but he did not return their greeting. Fear thrummed in the veins in his hands. He had no idea what he would find in the far stall.

He stopped at the end of the aisle, and craned forward, looking through the gloom at the form inside the last tiny room. The figure stood against the back of the stall beneath a shuttered window, arms outstretched. Caleb stepped forward. The thin halo of light from beneath the shutters began to define the figure. It was a man, his arms and legs held out and tied with ropes. He was facing the wall.

Another raspy breath came, and a soft groan.

"Ho there," said Caleb gently. "What is this?"

There was a sharp grunt, then an anguished sigh. Caleb walked into the stall. With each step, he could make out more of the features of the man. He was tall, muscular, with his head held straight as if defying his agony. There was another breath—familiar, and as such, disheartening.

"Gaddi," said Caleb.

Gaddi's head turned, and though Caleb could not see the eyes, he knew he recognized Caleb. Caleb reached out and touched his friend on the back. It was tacky with blood and opened with fresh lash marks.

Caleb felt his own breath, sharp in his throat. "Dear God, what brought you to this?"

Gaddi's voice was a gravelly whisper. "Get out of here. You don't want to be around when Master Whitley returns."

"What happened?"

"Ah!" said Gaddi, and the word full of anger, despair, and hopelessness. "You must know? Bastard's selling off Fern! My sister's going to a turpentine forest in Georgia!"

"Why?"

"Get out of here, fool!"

"Tell me what happened."

"She refused the master! So many years he's had his way with her when he pleased. But she decided, no more of it! He came last night to our cabin, and dragged her by her hair to the lane. She screamed and he slapped her. He said 'no wench shall dare fight me!' I ran out to my fence, and saw her there, kickin' and bitin', and saw him drive his fist into her until she couldn't fight no more. Then he took advantage of her. Right in the snow. Ripped her skirt off, climbed on her, burying himself in her like a hog in rut!"

Caleb braced his knees so he would not drop to the straw beneath him.

"When he was done he kicked her square in the head," said Gaddi. "Left her outside. We brought her back in and tended her, but she was bruised up fiercely. Ribs broken. This morning, he called us together, told us that disobedience was always handled severely. He'd sent word to his cousin in Georgia. Fern'll be taken there end of the week."

"Why are you beaten?"

"I slapped Master Whitley. God damn him!"

"God help you! What can I do?"

"Nothing, Caleb. Just leave!"

Caleb swallowed, hard. There really was nothing he could do. Gaddi was a slave. Caleb was a free black with nothing of consequence but freeman's papers.

There the banging sound of the door opening, and then coughing at the front of the barn. There was a flicker of lantern light. Caleb ran to hide behind a bale of hay in the aisle. He crouched down, clutching the prickly blades of dried grass. His heart pounded so loudly he was certain whoever had come into the barn would hear it. How could he get out without being seen? But he couldn't leave Gaddi here alone, to face more torture.

The man walked toward the hay bale, causing Caleb to pull down even farther as the light pooled across the aisle and walls, and then turned into the stall where Gaddi was tied. It was Mr. Whitley, and the stench of whiskey on the man was stronger than any manure in the barn. He teetered on his feet, but the sound of his voice was deadly.

"There you be, you insolent blackie. You may be quick in a slave fight, but you are naught against me! Where's my crop, now? Ah, here. Time for another lesson. And you will have a lesson every day until you die from the blows, or until I have beat the willfulness from your brazen soul!"

Mr. Whitley put the lantern on a hook, and leaned down to pull the crop from the top of his boot. Caleb watched the man move as if in a bad dream, knowing what was going to happen next, knowing Gaddi would be flayed alive, his skin ripped like peeling from an apple, and knowing he could not stand for it. Regardless of the aftermath.

He rushed upward with a cry and raced into the stall, slamming the white man with his forearms and knocking him to the straw. Mr. Whitley roared like a bull, and tried to roll over on his fat belly, but Caleb jumped on the man's back and grabbed at his hair. It came off the man's head; a wig. Caleb hurled it aside and began pounding the man about the neck and skull. Gaddi began to shout, "No! No!" but Caleb could not stop. His hands flew against the dreaded master, causing the man to gurgle and shake.

"Stop it now!" cried Gaddi.

Caleb's mind whirled as he struck. He remembered fighting Jeremiah Martin for untrue words, he remembered Gaddi fighting Tall Jim for new shoes. He remembered chipmunks fighting each other for territory, and Flash fighting the vicious tangle of locust thorns on the creek bank.

"Caleb!"

Caleb beat the man several more times, then slowly slid off the man's back. Mr. Whitley did not move.

"Oh, God," moaned Caleb.

"You've killed him?" asked Gaddi.

"No, he's breathing. But he's done in, and terribly so."

"We'll be hanged!" said Gaddi. "Grundy will see that we dance from a tree branch in the mouth of a rope!"

Caleb's head was ringing, and as he stood, he felt the earth rolling beneath him. What had he done? He'd sworn to no violence for the rest of his days! Surely God was preparing a place in hell for him at this very moment!

"We have to run away!" said Gaddi. "Untie me, Caleb, now, or we'll be killed for certain!"

Caleb stared at the man on the floor. He grabbed the man's mitted hands, with hopes that he could drag him deeper into the stall corner that he would not be found as quickly.

The fat man didn't budge. The mitts slipped off

in Caleb's grasp. And in the lantern light, Caleb saw a truth he never could have imagined.

Both hands were paddle-paws. Both sets of the last three fingers were fused at the knuckles. The man wore mitts constantly to hide his deformity. Caleb's deformity. The curse of the hawk. But clearly it had not been a hawk that had swooped down on Caleb's mother so many years ago.

It had been a fat, sweaty tobacco master.

Mr. Whitley must have found her as she had been walking alone on the road in search for her sister Onnie, and had taken advantage of her as he had done Fern.

"Untie me!" hissed Gaddi.

Caleb fell back against the stall wall, staring at the man on the floor. His eyes bugged.

"Caleb!" said Gaddi.

Mr. Whitley is my father.

"Hurry, Caleb!"

Mr. Whitley is my father! Oh, God, I should die this moment and never have to think on this appalling thing!

"Caleb!"

Caleb fell toward Gaddi, and with trembling fingers fumbled out the knots at his wrists and then at his ankles. The air was thick, so thick he could hardly catch his breath. He felt he would drown in the air, the way his mother used to say he would drown in the river if he went in too deep. He gasped, his lungs straining with the effort. He tasted straw dust and terror in his nostrils and mouth.

The ropes were at last free from Gaddi, and the slave took Caleb by the arm. "Put out the lantern and follow me."

Caleb blew out the lantern, then the two men scurried down the aisle of the barn, past the curious horses, and peered out of the door.

Night had fallen completely. The slaves were back from the fields, moving up the lane toward the cabins. In but a moment, the overseer Grundy and his men would be at the barn, to bed their mounts and report to Mr. Whitley.

"Come!" whispered Gaddi urgently. He pulled Caleb out of the barn. They fell in with the marching slaves to the surprised utterances of some but then the knowing, protective silence of the crowd. Caleb could see the faces of others as they moved en masse, and knew they could read the urgency on his. They couldn't know what he and Gaddi had planned, but they would do nothing to give the secret away.

Behind the slaves was the sound of hoof beats, and the laughter of Grundy and his fellow overseers as they drew up their horses by the barn. Caleb dipped down, keeping close to Gaddi, as the two wormed their way through the slaves to the edge of the crowd. Over the knoll they went, and when they reached the apple orchard, Gaddi shoved Caleb into the tangle of leafless branches and gnarled trunks, where the two dropped and rolled and then lay still in a low spot on the ground where a thicket of brambles hid them from view.

They lay silently for a moment, panting in pain and exhaustion, and then Gaddi nudged Caleb. He tipped his head. It was time to run. They scooted along the ground between the trees of the orchard, and then reached the rail fencing at the edge of the forest. They climbed the fence and pushed into the thick cluster of trees. Gaddi grunted and wheezed, the cruel wounds on his back making his escape excruciating.

They ran. They tripped over logs, vines, stones. An owl wailed in the darkness, a wolf howled in the distance. The land sloped downward, becoming muddier and more difficult to traverse. Caleb stumbled in the too-small boots, twisting his ankle painfully, but forced himself onward.

Where are we going? Where is there to go? We shall be caught, surely, and we shall hang!

They at last came to the rolling road which lead west to Adam Donaughby's farm. Gaddi turned and grabbed Caleb by the wrist. Sweat flew from his face like flies. His hand was hot as a branding iron. "Go home, Caleb! They'd be out now, getting the hounds together to hunt me down. Go home!"

"I can't," managed Caleb. "I have no home!"

"What?" cried Gaddi, but then took no time to ask for there was no time to spare. He ran across the road and into the forest. With a wail of anguish, Caleb followed his friend.

❧ 17 ❧

CALEB'S FEET WERE cramped and raw, his ankle throbbing, yet in the hours since they'd run from River's Pine they had covered no more than seven miles, Caleb was certain. They fell at last to rest on a pebbly creek bank. It was a secluded spot, shaded by pine trees and protected by a steep hill on the west side. As the sun rose from behind the trees in the east, Caleb and Gaddi sat on in silence, tossing pebbles into the creek. The only sounds were the plunking of the pebbles in the water and the chirping of birds overhead as they awakened for the day.

Thank God there are no hounds baying. Maybe we will be safe, after all. Then he shook his head balefully. *And maybe I am just full of fanciful thoughts.*

Gaddi broke the silence. "I'm sorry, Caleb. Got you in this and I don't know how to go back and make it right."

"It's too late to change anything," said Caleb.

Gaddi dashed water from the creek onto his face. He rubbed it over his cheeks and neck. Caleb could see the wounds on his back clearly now. There were twenty-two deep gashes, the length of a forearm. Jesus had been lashed not much more than this. Gaddi, dressed only in trousers, had nothing with which to bind the wounds. Caleb remembered the extra shirt he had in his sack, and made to reach for it, and then stopped cold.

"No!" he wailed. "I left my sack at the barn! They will look inside and know it was me there with you! They will know there are two of us!"

Gaddi threw another pebble into the creek.

Caleb removed his jacket then his shirt. He handed it to Gaddi, then put his jacket back on. Gaddi eased on the shirt, grimacing silently as he did. It was too small to button in front.

"So are you gonna go with me to Virginia, Caleb?" he asked at last.

"Virginia? Why Virginia?"

"There's a man named Dunmore in Norfolk, once a Virginia governor and now a British Naval officer in the Chesapeake Bay, who's offered freedom to any Negro who will fight by his side. Alice told Fern 'bout it. Alice works in the big house, and Fern helps her with the washing. Alice hears lots of white folk talk."

"You don't even know how to find Virginia."

"I do. It's south. I'm gonna fight for the Redcoats. I'm gonna fight with the men of the King. I'm gonna help win the war 'gainst the colonists who own slaves. When the fightin' is over, I'm gonna be free. Then I'll find Fern, buy her, and set her free, too."

Caleb threw another pebble into the stream. How simple to be a pebble or a drop of water. You would just be what you were, with no concern of doing something wrong.

"You want to come fight, too?"

"I have nowhere to go. I have nothing."

"That's all I have," said Gaddi. "But now I'm gonna fight for something bigger than just me."

Caleb sighed, and he said, "We gotta sleep. We can't stay here long, but we'll get nowhere else if we don't rest."

The two lay down on the damp creek bank. Caleb cushioned his head on his forearm. A few hours of sleep would do. Then they could follow this stream. Streams became rivers, he knew. And rivers, he'd learned from his mother, flowed to the great and mighty sea. Perhaps even the Chesapeake Bay.

I am bound to Virginia with an escaped slave, he thought, *to join a naval officer I know nothing about.* He stared at the sky above him. In the morning clouds he saw disjointed images of horses and muskets and hand wraps flying like flags; of paddle-paws and Charity's weeping face and a man lying unconscious in a dark stall.

Caleb closed his fingers together around an imaginary pen and wrote in the air:

God has taken everything from me. My mother. My home. A girl I cared for. The chance to work for pay at River's Pine. If He has taken all this, there must be a reason. All my life I've learned that God's ways are mysterious and we should walk in faith.

My destiny is sealed. I have no choice but to go where I am going.

Caleb paused to stare at the creek and the skim of leaves atop the water, drifting southward without a care. Without a mother, save the tree that bore them; without honor or lack of honor, without pride or anger or duty.

Mr. Whitley attacked my mother. My father is not a hero, he is a devil.

Caleb closed his eyes for a moment and grit his teeth against the terrible truth. It was no wonder Fern recoiled at the touch of Caleb's hand; she had seen hands like that before, in the secret, dark times the devil had violated her. He opened his eyes, and on the clouds he wrote:

Whitley is a devil. Surely God knows that it would have been more of a sin to let the devil beat Gaddi to death than to use my power to stop him.

But then, something stirred, then welled in his heart, something that for a moment, canceled out the fatigue of his body and mind. He remembered the story of the *Peggy Stewart,* and how he had imagined himself forcing Mr. Whitley into the sea, helping to free the slaves. Helping to free his brothers. In the air he wrote:

God help me, I will join the British with Gaddi and fight to my death against men such as Whitley. It is right that I am here, and it is right to go to Virginia and join Dunmore. I am not a leaf on the water. I am a man. A man makes his decision. A man does what is right.

And I will belong. God help me, I shall belong!

Caleb struggled back to consciousness and prodded Gaddi awake. It had begun to rain lightly. Caleb wiped water from his face and wished he had a cloak large enough for his frame, one he could wrap around his body to keep out the damp. He and Gaddi sipped water from the creek, tried to push back the growling of their empty stomachs, and started off again for Virginia's coast far away.

But the creek was impossible to track in places; the land rose and fell in severe, rocky cliffs and pitted hollows, and undergrowth was so dense at times it would have taken an axe to open it. And so Caleb and Gaddi found themselves splashing down lengths of the stream at times, arms outstretched to keep upright on the slick stones of the creek bottom. Caleb's ankle complained. The too-tight boots pinched dreadfully, making his toes and heels burn.

Occasionally they came upon an open stretch of land, and they could see fields plowed for tobacco, barns and cabins. Once a large brown dog guarding a field of cattle spied them and made chase into the trees. Gaddi and Caleb threw rocks at the dog as they ran, and then in desperation Caleb took off one of his boots and flung it behind him. He was relieved to look back seconds later to see the animal hunched over the leather, chewing at it as if he'd made a kill. The dog's attention was distracted long enough for Gaddi and Caleb to get to the stream and hop into it, extinguishing their scents. The chill of the water bit into Caleb's bare foot like briars. Now he had one freezing foot and one bad ankle, a poor combination for a long trip.

Another hour passed, and another. They lost the stream, found it again, and this time it was wider and deeper.

Walking after sunset was difficult since Caleb and Gaddi had neither lantern nor torch. Besides stealthy slave catchers, Caleb began to worry about other things he couldn't see. Wolves. Rattlesnakes. As was true the night before, they found themselves tripping and scraping their hands on the bark of trees. Gaddi cursed and Caleb began to curse, too, something he'd never been allowed to do.

The creek at last emptied into a large river.

"This must be the Patapsco," Caleb told Gaddi. He knew tobacco planters rolled their hogsheads to this river, where there were settlements and riverside warehouses. Caleb wished he had a map. He suddenly felt more helpless than he ever had in his life. And helplessness made him angry.

"Damn my empty stomach and heavy eyelids!" he cursed.

A short distance along the river they reached a bridge and a road. Standing behind a patch of trees, they stared at the bridge for a few moments. Then, Gaddi said what Caleb had been thinking. "Not many travel the roads at night, am I right? Why don't we take the road? We can be careful."

It sounded dangerous. Slave catchers, after a shilling bag, would not care if it was day or night. But Caleb was too weary to argue. "If we hear anything, any movement at all even if it sounds no more than a mouse," said Caleb, "will you jump quick as a fox into the trees?"

"Do you think I won't? Don't talk to me like a child."

"I'm sorry. I'm cross and tired."

The flat surface of the bridge was kind beneath Caleb's boot and bare foot. He swung his arms, working the cramps out of his shoulders. Below him, he could hear the water rushing over rocks and fallen logs.

Gaddi's arms didn't swing so boldly. He glanced furtively to the left and right. He had never walked in the open without a master or overseer behind him with a whip.

On the other side of the bridge the road turned south. The river traveled along the roadside just below a line of brush and small trees. And then, the road went downhill slightly and the trees opened up. Gaddi and Caleb stopped in their tracks. There before them were several stone buildings, side by side. Smoke came from the chimneys and both lights and voices came through the windows.

Immediately, Caleb and Gaddi jumped into the trees. Caleb peered back out, but Gaddi would not. "What is that?" Gaddi asked. "Is it a slave catchers' gathering place?"

"Shhh," whispered Caleb.

"We got to get back in the woods," said Gaddi.

But Caleb caught a whiff of meat cooking. His stomach began to grumble loudly. His mouth began to water.

You can catch something to eat in the morning, he told himself. *A fish. A frog. It'll take time, but you can do it.*

The scent from the stone house was that of roasted pork, joined by smells of onions and freshly baked bread. As Caleb watched, a woman in a white apron and cap came out the door of the house to the yard. She dumped something from a large pan into a pile. Immediately, two large sows ambled from behind a lean-to and began to feed.

Scraps, Caleb thought. *Scraps of bread or vegetables!*

"Caleb, c'mon!" hissed Gaddi.

"No, wait," said Caleb. "Stay there out of sight. I shall fetch us something to eat."

"You won't!"

"I'll be back in an eye's wink. No one shall see me or hear me. The rain will cover any sound I make."

"Don't! You'll put us at risk!"

But Caleb was already skirting the rim of trees, leaping the picket fence and dropping behind a woodpile at the side of the house. The sows had noticed him and grunted angrily as if they knew he had designs on their meal.

Suddenly something bumped into Caleb's shoulder. Startled, he looked around to see Gaddi crouched with him behind the logs. He said nothing, but gave Caleb a strained expression that said, "I'll get my own food, thank you."

Holding as low as they could, they moved around the woodpile and toward the scraps. There were onions here, and the scent of burned pork fat made Caleb's mouth water. Not far now, and they would take their dinner and run. The sows bolted off and stood grunting several feet away.

"Ah," whispered Gaddi. "Not the good food from back at the quarters, but it smells good all the same."

Caleb and Gaddi knelt beside the pile and began to pick the best pieces of scraps and stuck them into their shirts.

Pork fat, Caleb thought. *Burned beans! A feast, truly!*

And then there was the tip of a sword pressed against the back of Caleb's head, and a man saying, "What have we here? Two thieves, by God!"

Caleb froze in place. Beside him, Gaddi did the same.

"Get up, boys, and let's have a look at ye!"

Caleb and Gaddi dropped the soggy handfuls of scorched beans and slowly stood up. They turned around.

There stood a large man with a broad face, a thick beard, and a huge scowl. The sword shook as if he did not truly want to use it. "Who are ye boys?" he bellowed.

Caleb couldn't find his voice. What was he to

say? He couldn't tell the truth, but he'd not taken time to think up an appropriate lie. He had his freeman's paper in his jacket, but his name might be his doom, for who knew how far word had spread of the attack on Mr. Whitley?

"Are ye deaf and dumb? Speak!" shouted the man.

There were others now, pouring out the door of the house and gathering around. Their clothing was simple, suggesting they were Quakers. There were five men and two women.

"Speak!" demanded the man with the sword. "Or I'll be forced to lock you in the tool house!"

"Well, well!" came a second man's voice from the right. Caleb didn't dare look away from the man with the sword, but he had an odd feeling that he'd heard this voice before.

"What?" asked the man with the sword.

"Gracious, Jonathan Ellicott, I know this young man."

The sword wobbled a little with uncertainty. "Indeed?"

"Unless my eyes are failing me more quickly than the rest of my body, he's an apprentice to Adam Donaughby."

Caleb looked to see who it was who spoke. And he was stunned to see Mr. Benjamin Banneker, the man who had spoken so kindly to him two years prior at the tavern.

"Indeed?" asked Jonathan Ellicott.

"Ah yes," said Mr. Banneker. "I invited him to come visit if he ever found the time. He took me at my word, I see."

The sword went down and hung in Mr. Ellicott's grip. The women whispered to each other behind their hands, and the men continued to frown behind their beards. "It is night and the air misty with rain. Look closer. Are thee certain that thou knows this lad?"

"He is Caleb Jacobson. Speak up, Caleb."

"It is a pleasure to meet you, Mr. Ellicott," Caleb said. He bowed slightly and put out his hand, which was filthy with pig slop. Mr. Ellicott took it gingerly and then let it go. Caleb felt as if he were in the middle of a dream. He was covered with mud and blood, wearing only one boot, and had been found digging for scraps in a pig's heap. And yet he was having to act as though nothing were out of the ordinary, as if he had just arrived after a pleasant journey to pay a friendly visit to Benjamin Banneker.

"Well, then," said Mr. Banneker. "Welcome to Ellicott Mills. I must say I am surprised thee came on such a cold night, and with no provisions. Not even a second boot."

"Sir, I . . . ," began Caleb. What could he say?

"And thy companion?"

Even if word had not come about the attempt on Mr. Whitley, soon it would, and if Gaddi's name was out, he could be tracked from here. "His name is Galen," said Caleb, catching the sight of the stone house. "Galen Stone."

Jonathan Ellicott made an exasperated sound. "Look at the boys, Benjamin! They act and dress as thieves." There was a moment of silence all around the yard, with only the sounds of the pigs grunting and the river running south, tumbling across the stones at the fall line over the embankment.

Then, his voice steady and calm, Benjamin said, "My friends, Jesus stands at the door and knocks humbly. He says he who does it unto the least of these does it also until Him. These boys may look like the least, but I did invite young Mr. Jacobson to visit me, and he is here. That is good enough for me. I need know no more."

The people looked at each other. They shifted from foot to foot. Caleb shivered beneath his too-small jacket.

"Thee indeed are correct, Benjamin," said one woman, smiling suddenly. She came forward and took Caleb by the arm. Another woman took Gaddi's arm. "Forgive our hesitation. The Lord commands we look after thee, and give thee food and shelter. Come inside and share our meal."

Caleb and Gaddi let themselves be escorted into the warm stone house.

❧ 18 ❧

THE ELLICOTT HOUSE was plainly furnished yet roomy. After shedding their shoes and boot, Caleb and Gaddi were sat by the fireplace on a rug and given bowls of steaming beans, potatoes, and chunks of beef and mugs of ale. Caleb was aware the Quakers wanted to ask more of them, but they kept their questions to themselves. The women returned to needlework and the men sat around the fire, talking about the science of surveying. Words like "meridian," "sectors," and "nutation" confounded Caleb, and, unable to concentrate because of his lack of understanding, he found the drone of the voices putting him to sleep. He wavered, his eyes closing, then jerked awake as one of the men threw another log on the fire.

Mr. Banneker must have noticed the sleepiness of his guests, because he rose from his chair. "I come to buy flour and an axe head from thy store this afternoon and end up spending many hours talking. I must take my leave now, friends, and see to my company."

Gaddi and Caleb offered farewells to the Ellicott family and slipped on their footwear. The younger Ellicott son, George, asked Caleb to wait a moment and he left the room. He returned with a pair of scuffed but intact shoes. "These might serve thee better than the one," he said. Caleb thanked him and slipped the shoes on. They fit fine.

"My home is not far over the ridge," said Banneker as they walked out into the night. He went to the far side of the house and came back with his mount. Mr. Banneker swung into his saddle and collected his reins. Then he rode ahead, across the road and up a well-worn trail through the trees. Caleb and Gaddi followed on foot, too tired to talk. Caleb could not remember a time when he was more weary, but his feet, thrilled to be wearing something which fit, kept up with the white-haired man and his horse.

Less than thirty minutes later, they emerged from the hilly forest into a hilly pasture with a cabin set on a level plot. The rain had stopped and the clouds in the night sky were beginning to break up. Moonlight pooled over the pasture land and the furrowed rows. Mr. Banneker's horse picked a narrow path through the field to the cabin. There was a single candle burning in the window.

"My mother waits for me," Benjamin said as he slipped out of his saddle and ran the stirrups up the leathers. "I live with her and she is advanced in years." He lead his mount to a paddock beside a small tool barn, took off her saddle and bridle, gave her a pat on the flank, then came back to the cabin with the tack. But before he opened the front door, he looked back at Caleb and Gaddi and said, "We shall wait until morning to visit. I do not know what inspired this long journey from the Donaughby farm to Ellicott Mills, but I sense that thee have had little sleep in the last days."

They went inside.

Benjamin Banneker's mother was in a chair in the one-room cabin, seated next to the window and candle. As the flame flickered across her features she looked alternately like a young girl and a weathered matron. "Benjamin, we've guests?" she asked. Her voice was soft yet strong.

"I give you Caleb Jacobson and Galen Stone, Mother."

The old woman nodded and held up her hand in greeting. "So pleased to make your acquaintance," she said. And then, "Benjamin, I will retire now that thee are home safely."

"Good night," said Benjamin. "Sleep well."

The old woman pulled herself slowly out of the chair, shuffled to a corner on her bare feet and lay down on a cot. She pulled the blanket under her chin and rolled to face the wall. Mr. Banneker lit another candle from the coals in the fireplace. He put it on a table and sat down to take off his boots. "I will get blankets for thee," he said. " 'Tis warm by the fire and thy clothes can dry as thee sleep. Is there anything thee need before retiring?"

"No, sir," said Caleb. Then he noticed a fine-looking clock on the mantle over the fireplace. Neither Caleb nor the Donaughbys owned a clock. Only Mr. Donaughby had a small pocket watch. "That is a fine instrument," Caleb said.

"Thank thee," said Mr. Banneker.

By the time the clock on the mantle read five past ten, Gaddi was snoring on the floor in his blanket, Mr. Banneker was snoring on his cot, and

Caleb was feeling his own mind giving up the ghost to the warmth of the cabin.

"Benjamin made that clock when he was twenty-two years of age," said Mary Banneker, Benjamin's mother. She was in the yard in her black dress and white bonnet, cooking fat down to make soap in a large pot. After a night's sleep she was not frail but a strong and feisty old female. "People came from all over the Hollow and beyond to see. They couldn't believe a black man had done such a thing. Benjamin borrowed a watch and studied it. Then, with the workings in his mind he set out to make a large clock based on what he'd seen. But the time he spent, drawing diagrams of wheels and gears, carving pieces, fitting them together, refitting until it was right. It keeps perfect time!"

"Yes, ma'am," said Caleb and Gaddi together.

Mr. Banneker, Caleb, and Gaddi were seated on a wooden bench outside the cabin. Caleb and Gaddi had slept late, waking only when they heard chopping outside. Mr. Banneker had been cutting wood. His mother was weeding potato hills. After Caleb and Gaddi had put on their dry clothes, Mr. Banneker offered them a breakfast of biscuits and jam. Now, Mr. Banneker was sharpening his axe head and Caleb was wondering how much he dared say about his predicament.

"Could we walk your farm, sir?" asked Caleb.

Mr. Banneker lay his axe and whetstone aside. "Certainly." He brushed himself off and strolled across the small yard to the path through the field. Caleb and Gaddi followed.

"What do you grow, sir?" Gaddi asked.

"Tobacco," said Mr. Banneker. "It is my cash

crop. This year I will plant a large amount of wheat, also."

Mr. Banneker walked slowly, his head down, his broad-brimmed hat shading his eyes. He said nothing more, as if he was waiting for Caleb to speak his mind.

And so Caleb began, "I believe I can trust you, sir. You were more than fair to us last night."

Mr. Banneker paused to pick up an earthworm and toss it into the soft soil off the path.

"I must be honest, this visit was not planned."

"No?"

"No, sir, and I'm certain you knew that. Gaddi . . . Galen and I are fugitives. We are going south to Norfolk, Virginia, to join with Lord Dunmore's troops. He issued a proclamation that any black who joins his ranks will be given his freedom at the conclusion of the war."

"I have read that proclamation," said Mr. Banneker. "Issued last December. But how are you a fugitive?"

"Galen is an escaped slave."

"I see," said Mr. Banneker. He reached the far side of pasture, and began to walk along the edge of the woods. Now, the three could travel side-by-side. "I've lived in this area my whole life," the man said. "My grandmother came to Maryland from England as an indentured servant, a lone woman banished from her country for spilling a pail of milk. She served her seven years then came into the wilderness and raised tobacco. She bought two slaves, married one of them, and founded my family. I have always held high esteem for those who do what they must to survive. I understand and respect men who must face an enemy to gain what is rightfully theirs and what is rightfully their neighbor's."

"Yes, sir," said Gaddi.

"I've lived free my whole life, though free is a relative term, is it not, Caleb? And I've seen the suffering of my slave brothers on the rolling roads. I fear for thee, Galen, but I cannot say I would not do as you, were I thee."

"Thank you, sir."

"Thee will be on thy way, then," said Mr. Banneker. "But how can I help before thee go?"

"Have you paper and ink?" asked Caleb. "I could write a note to make Galen free."

Mr. Banneker turned around to look at the two. His eyes were kind but sad, as if he knew the risks they faced. But he said, "You may have paper, pen, and ink. And take some with you on your journey if you happen upon the opportunity to write me at some time."

Back in the cabin, Caleb sat at the window at Mr. Banneker's table, and dipped a quill pen into a bottle of ink. Gaddi stood at Caleb's shoulder, breathing down his ear. He was dressed in a shirt Mr. Banneker had given him to replace the too-small one he'd been wearing.

Caleb wrote, *March 31st, 1776.*

"What's that say?" asked Gaddi.

"It tells the day. Today. March 31st."

Caleb dipped the pen again, and wrote:

Let it be known that the Negro male Galen, age twenty-one years, is given his freedom for his years of good work service. This is done by my own hand and will, and thus I grant Galen the rights of a free-born Negro.

"And that?" asked Gaddi.

Caleb read the statement.

"Now sign it Dr. Oliver Taylor," said Gaddi.

"That sounds like an honest name, doesn't it?"

"It does," said Caleb. When the name was penned, he considered his handiwork. He had never used his skill for something illegal, and he felt a surge of fear and pride. He blew on the paper for a moment, then held it up. "Here it is," he said. "You are no longer the slave Gaddi. You are the freeman Galen."

Gaddi laughed out loud, then took the paper and gently folded it and put it into his shirt. "God be praised!" he said. "No one can send me back to River's Pine no more!"

"Time to leave," said Caleb. He opened a leather satchel Mr. Banneker had given him and put into it a pen, ink bottle, and handful of paper. The he added the bundles of bread and ham and a small pouch of coins Mrs. Banneker had insisted he take as well as Caleb's own freeman's paper.

They went outside and paused in front of the cabin. Mr. Banneker continued to chop wood as Caleb approached, then stopped and leaned the axe against a log. He gave Caleb a long look that was understanding and cautionary.

"Godspeed," he said at last. "Keep thy courage, but let wisdom, not passion, be your counsel."

"Thank you, sir," said Caleb. "Continued good health to you and your mother, and may your crops do well."

"A good amount of the grain I raise will go to the Colonial Army and their brave soldiers," said Mr. Banneker, stretching his hand out toward the furrowed ground. "They have few provisions, and I must do what I can. These men are fighting against the oppression of a cruel king."

It felt as though Caleb had been slapped.

"Sometimes it is the greater good toward which

we should aim, the good for the greatest number," said Mr. Banneker. "Sometimes we must have patience, and look further than a dark moment to see the brighter future."

Caleb didn't know what to say. His heart raced. This man was supporting the fight of those who owned slaves and who even made life difficult for a free black! It was the same as if he'd said he was raising crops for Mr. Whitley!

"Sir," Caleb stammered. But then he said, "Farewell, sir. And thank you for your kindness."

Mr. Banneker shook Gaddi's hand and then went back to the chopping. Caleb slung the leather satchel over his arm and he and Gaddi left the Banneker farm for the woods.

As his feet pounded the ground, the blood pounded in his ears. A black man supporting the colonists! It made no sense to him. Slaves were forbidden to fight for the side of the colonists. Caleb had heard Mr. Donaughby say that Washington was afraid the blacks, once armed, would rise up and kill their fellow soldiers. Why, then, would a black *want* to risk his life for such a general? Why would a free black with a large tobacco farm use half of his land to raise food for this general's army?

"What is on your mind?" asked Gaddi.

"Finding a map so we can find Virginia. Gaddi, I fear we shall waste a great deal of time and shall wear a great deal of shoe leather if we don't find a map."

"Where can we get a map?"

"Nowhere I can think of."

"Why're you angry?"

"I am not angry, Gaddi. Galen."

"Then slow down. We don't need to run. We got papers."

"Do you wish to get to Virginia as soon as possible? If I allowed you to, we'd be shuffling like Mary Banneker. By the time we got to Norfolk, the war would be over!"

Gaddi slammed the heels of his hands into Caleb's back, sending him flying into the leaves and pine silt.

Caleb rolled over, spitting out dirt. "You shoved me!"

"Thank me for it. It stopped you from acting a fool! Now get up, be quiet, and let's find us a road to the south!"

Caleb clambered up with Gaddi's help, and brushed off the knees of his breeches. There was a rip in the right leg. "You don't happen to have needle and thread with you?"

"Oh, yes, I just happen to have that. Had 'em in my trousers when Master went to whipping me in the barn, since you never know when you might be in the need to sew."

Caleb sighed deeply. "I'm sorry," he said.

And they began walking once more.

❧ 19 ❧

"IT WOULD BE best to find a road," said Galen as they worked their way through the trees. "We've got papers. If we act scared, runnin' in the woods all the time an' gettin' cut up, we gonna look like runaways. If we take roads, but act humble, we might slip by safely."

"There's no guarantee we won't be stopped," said Caleb.

"No. But ain't no guarantees in life, anyway."

Galen was right, Caleb knew.

Fifteen minutes later they found Ellicott's road east of the mills, and an hour later a rolling road traveling south. What towns or communities they would pass they weren't certain. But south meant Virginia. They did not hold their heads up for fear of appearing pompous. But Caleb held his heart up in hope. They passed merchants and slaves pulling and pushing huge rolling hogsheads toward Baltimore, and farmers on the roads herding sheep and goats, some of whom ignored them as if they were no more than oxen or dogs, and others who demanded to see their papers, then let them go.

And, as if God was answering, as if God Himself thought it might be all right for Caleb and Gaddi to get to Norfolk after all, there came down the road a wagon with a white family—a father, mother, and two children. In the back were barrels, crates, and bundles, with tattered blankets and a few cooking pots. The man at the reins gave the couple on the road no more than a passing glance, and this gave Caleb an idea.

"Sir!" he called, dipping his head respectfully. "May I have a moment?"

The man drew his horse up and turned in his seat. The wife, holding a baby in her arms and a child on her lap, squinted. "What do you want, boy?" the man asked. He had a poorly shaved face with road dirt caught in the creases.

"We have business in Virginia. We are horse trainers from Baltimore, sent for by a planter in Norfolk. Mr. Randolph Bonnie. Perhaps you know of him? We'd thought of sparing our shillings by walking but it proves to be a much greater endeavor than we had imagined. Would you consider giving us space in the back of your wagon?"

"Puh!" said the man. "I've no reason to trust Negroes!"

"I've shillings. I would be happy to give you all I have for a ride south if you are going that way."

Caleb could almost read Galen's mind, "All you have you give for a ride? Don't do it!"

"Do you now?" asked the man. "I am to believe that?"

"Yes, sir," said Caleb, still looking at the ground.

"Show me what you have," said the man.

Caleb opened the pouch Mr. Banneker had

given him, and held up the coins. The wife shifted in her seat, looking weary but interested. The baby in her arms squirmed. The little boy in her lap snuggled closer to his mother.

"We are going to Williamsburg," said the man. "Not Norfolk. A five day's journey. You would knock us in the head and rob us!"

"Sir, we would pay, and even allow you to bind our hands if it would make you more comfortable. We seek only a ride."

Galen's eyes widened.

"Rufus," said the woman. "We could use the extra money."

"Puh!" said Rufus.

"We can bind their hands!" said the wife.

The man hawked over the side of the wagon to the road. Then he said, "Give me! I've a sharp hunting knife! Don't think I won't use it if need be."

Caleb handed the man the money, and the man counted it three times before stashing it inside a pouch at his feet. "Get in, then," he said. "Put your hands out. Millie, use some of that hemp to secure them."

Galen hesitated, but Caleb gave him a nod and climbed into the rear of the wagon. Slowly, Galen climbed in, too. They both settled down between a stack of crates and a large barrel. As the horse was urged back into motion, the woman handed the baby to the little boy and leaned over, taking two pieces of rope and tying Caleb's wrists together, then doing the same to Galen. As she turned back around, she said, "And don't let us hear jabber back there!"

It was a good five minutes before Galen could find his voice. He leaned forward and in an urgent whisper said, "This is a damned lunatic's idea!"

Caleb said, "We will make it to Virginia now."

"But you've spent all your money!"

"Not all. Some is in my shoe. My mother taught me to never keep all my money in one place."

"But our hands are bound!"

"Not so tightly. And there may be other advantages not yet seen. We've got ourselves a disguise."

"What do you mean?"

"They're jabbering, Mama!" said the little boy. Caleb looked at the front of the wagon. The boy was turned around, his arms folded across the back of the seat. His eyes were little sparkles beneath the brim of his hat.

"You two hush!" said Rufus.

Galen slumped against the barrel and closed his eyes.

Later that evening, as night draped its foggy cloak over the land and Caleb and Galen were cramped and restless from sitting in limited positions with hands bound, there came from behind a pair of riders, moving up quickly, the sound of the hoofbeats like thunder from the north.

This is it, Caleb thought. *It had to happen sooner or later. I suspect these men are looking for escaped slaves. I hear it in the urgency of their horses.*

The men slowed as they approached the wagon, and when beside it, glared inside. They were rough-looking men with haughty eyes. They carried muskets and swords on their backs. Their horses frothed at the mouth.

Caleb purposefully shifted his position slightly so the ropes on his wrists were visible in the moonlight. Then he looked humbly at his lap. The men both took stock of the bound Negroes, grunted to each other, and rode up beside the couple in front. "Pull up!" demanded one.

Rufus clucked to his horse, urging it on faster.

"Pull up!" The man rode beside the harnessed horse and caught hold of the cheek strap, forcing the horse to stop.

"Let go!" said Rufus. "You've no business with us!"

"We do, indeed!" said the second man.

"Let go of our horse!" said the little boy.

"Make the brat hush, woman," said the first man. "And listen to us. We are seeking two escaped slaves."

Rufus slapped the reins against the back of his horse, but the animal was still held by the strap and could not move far. It danced in place.

"Talk to us, old man!" said the first rider. "We seek two escaped slaves, attempted murderers they are!"

"Nearly killed a planter west of Baltimore. Man won't wake up," said the second rider. "He's hired us to track them down. Have you seen two young blackies, well-worn for their travels, no doubt?"

"How could he hire you if he can't wake?" asked the wife.

"Woman!" said the first rider. "His wife hired us, then, his family. Does it matter?"

"Let us go," said Rufus.

"Have you seen two escaped darkies?"

"No," said Earl. "Let us go!"

"Are you certain?"

"Do you call me a liar?" asked Rufus. "Leave us!"

"Very well, then," said the first man. He at last let go of the horse's cheek strap. "Good evening, sir, madam." The two men grudgingly tipped their hats, urged their horses to a gallop, and disappeared around the bend in the road.

"Suggesting we are liars!" spit Rufus. "They treated us as if we were escaped blackies, ourselves!"

"They did, indeed!" said the wife.

At long last the wagon pulled to the roadside. The family got down and stretched. Galen whispered to Caleb. "You thought well, Caleb! The catchers saw us as slaves of these people, tossed in the back like leashed dogs. If not for the ropes, they might have suspected us."

Caleb nodded. The ruse had worked. Now all they had to do was be patient for four more days, then make it another day or two from Williamsburg to Norfolk.

And hope the white people would spare a few crumbs of food and cups of water along the way if the food Mrs. Banneker had given them ran out.

❧ 20 ❧

THE DISTANCE FROM Williamsburg to Norfolk was longer than Caleb had guessed. After leaving the Rufus Scott family, they were back on foot, and walked three full days eastward in search of the sea and the bay city. They stayed clear of the well-traveled main road, collecting leaves of dandilions and cress for meals, and drinking what water they could find in rain puddles. They skirted farms and swampy stretches, sometimes spending entire hours in gullies with brush pulled atop themselves until it was safe to move on. They had freeman's papers, but the sight of a band of well-armed militia on the road as well as well-armed civilian scouts made Caleb know they should never be seen. Caleb's feet stung with open blisters, and his shoulders were cramped with anxiety and fatigue, but the closer they were to Norfolk, the more excited Galen became.

"Freedom is mostly mine," he said to Caleb as they hid themselves behind an outhouse a moment's rest. "I can taste it, can't you? I wish Fern could see .me! Better yet, I wish Master Whitley could see me!"

"Call him Mr. Whitley," said Caleb simply. "He is not your master anymore."

On the second morning, Caleb found a page of the *Virginia Gazette,* wet and plastered against a tree trunk. He peeled it carefully from the bark and scanned the articles. "What does that say?" asked Galen.

Caleb felt his stomach twist painfully as he read what it said. "This is about runaway slaves. It says they will be severely punished if caught, and that they should 'be content with their situation, and to expect a better condition in the next world.' Dunmore's call for slaves has frightened the slave owners. We must walk all the more softly than ever now that we are on Virginia soil."

Galen agreed solemnly. "But we don't have to be content with our situation."

Again, Caleb wished he'd had a map so he would know what lay ahead. But all he had was the sun, which rose and fell east to west. And the sea was east.

The road ended when the land did, in a town by the bay. Houses and shops stood clustered on side streets. Sea birds circled the air above the trees. Tall marsh grasses grew in wet, low-lying pastures. Caleb and Galen darted in and out among the inlets, gardens, barnyards, and white fences, staying out of sight, surprised that most of the houses seemed deserted, with no activity around or about them. A few seemed to be occupied by soldiers of the colonists, with officers on porches and a watch on duty in the yards.

Pausing behind a thick boxwood between an empty shop and a covered well, Caleb stared at a cluster of Continental soldiers by a roadside gate. They were not much older than Caleb, with uniforms of pale blue jackets, white waistcoats, white linen trousers, and black leggings. The hats were black felt with red bands and ratty plumes poking from them. He had seen a number of such soldiers from his roadside hiding places, in various degrees of uniform, but this was the first time he studied their faces. This was the enemy. These were those he was destined to fight with sword, arm, or rifle. He wondered what a battle would be like, and felt his blood jump beneath his skin, welcoming the battle.

At last Caleb and Galen made their way stealthily to the water's edge, and were able to see the full expanse, stretching out like an immense blue pasture, larger and more brilliant than anything Caleb had ever seen. And bobbing on the waves were countless ships of all sizes, with tall beams wrapped in white canvas rising from them. Caleb and Galen stared from a cluster of sticky cedars. Caleb felt suddenly afraid and small.

"What is all that?" whispered Galen. "Whose ships?"

It was then that Caleb recognized the British flag flying atop one of the larger vessels with overlaid crosses of blue, red, and white. He had seen sketches of this flag on notices tacked to the side of the King's Crown Tavern. The ships belonged to the King's men. And somehow, he and Galen would have to get aboard. "Dunmore's, I believe," he said.

Caleb and Galen scurried carefully into the yard of a tidy, empty brick house by the water's edge, and dropped behind the smokehouse.

"How we gonna cross to the ships?" Galen asked.

"Can't you swim?"

"No," said Galen. "Can you?"

"A bit," said Caleb. "But don't worry. I've seen our passage." He nodded to the rear of the house. There was a small sloping yard bordered with a picket fence. Just beyond the yard, jutting into the water amidst dense reeds and sedges, was a dock. Tethered to the dock was a small boat.

"We'll steal the boat," said Galen.

"We'll borrow the boat," said Caleb. "There is no commandment in the Bible against borrowing."

They hid until dark behind the smokehouse. They sat in the weeds, brushing away the gnats, listening to the marching feet of soldiers and the practice shots from a regiment not far away.

At last, Galen said, "Gon' now!"

They bolted across the side yard and into the back, leaping the white-washed fence. Immediately they were shin-deep in marshy water. Insects swirled into their faces and up their noses. Galen coughed and spit.

"I thought this was solid ground!" groaned Caleb as he and Galen pulled themselves onto the dock and shook off. Galen hopped into the boat and lifted a paddle. From the dock Caleb untied the rope, tossed it inside, and gave the boat a mighty push with his foot.

And then in the dark he could see Galen turning and his eyes widening. "Caleb!" he shouted. There was rustling grass and a shout of anger. Caleb spun about. A man was jumping onto the dock in the darkness, a wooden stick held aloft.

"Blackies flying to Dunmore, eh!" the man yelled. "And stealing my boat!" The stick whooshed in the air and Caleb ducked. Galen grabbed for the deck and tried to pull the boat back into place to help.

"Caleb!" he cried, fingers clutching.

The man swung the stick again. "I'll kill you and send your bodies back to your masters!"

Caleb ducked again, and slammed his head into the man's chest. The air left the man's lungs with a loud croak, and he stumbled backward onto the dock. But he held to the stick, and slashed it sideways. It cracked Caleb's ankles and he went down. The man was up then, lifting the stick and preparing to drive it downward like a pike. Caleb rolled aside and grabbed the bottom of the stick. He wrenched it sideways, and the man, refusing to let go, went down with it. Caleb jumped up and yanked the stick away.

"Kill him!" hissed Galen.

Caleb looked at the man on the deck. His face was contorted with fear and anger. Rage. Hate. In his mind he saw Mr. Whitley on the pier in Annapolis, and he was driving the man into the sea.

"Kill him!"

Caleb drove the stick down and into the man's chest. The man gasped, gurgled, and spewed blood. "No!" Caleb yelled, not believing what he had done. He kicked the man off the deck into the marshy, black water. He threw the stick in with him. The evidence of his crime, gone.

"Get in the boat!" said Galen.

Caleb gave the boat another shove and jumped in. He picked up a paddle and forced it into the weeds. His heart hammered in his throat, and he could smell blood in the night. His hands shook madly.

"How far out do these marshes go?" he managed.

"Can't see. Just paddle. Aim for the ships' lights!"

Caleb dug his paddle into the muck and reeds. The boat bobbed and moved ahead slowly. It reminded Caleb of when he was back at Adam Donaughby's farm, trying to walk through a deep snow after a winter storm. *What have I done?*

"Paddle, Caleb!"

Caleb blew air through his lips and strained on the paddle. And a few minutes later, they were out in open water, heading for the flickering lantern lights in the fleet of ships.

There was no wind to blow them back or work against them. The air was cool. The moon was full and cast a round yellow image on the rippling water's surface. Caleb felt it was a yellow cat's eye, evaluating him. And then, Caleb doubled up and vomited over the side of the boat. "Did I kill that man?" he said as he wiped his mouth when he was done.

"Yes, killed him good."

"I suppose I am truly a murderer now. I suppose I've done a great sin."

"You've done battle, Caleb," said Galen. "It is want you wanted, isn't it?"

Caleb couldn't answer.

❧ 21 ❧

THE CLOSEST SHIP rocked on the water, with only the glowing specks of lanterns making it visible through the night mist. Caleb and Galen stared as they moved through the brine-scented darkness. Damp air pelted their faces. The sound of the paddles and the waves slapping their tiny vessel was unbearably loud above the otherwise silent water.

Very slowly the night peeled back its layers to reveal the hulking sea monster, its silhouette black against shadowy gray. The ship was larger than Caleb had imagined the *Peggy Stewart,* and in his mind that ship had been enormous, indeed. Caleb felt bile from his empty stomach rise in his throat, but he swallowed it down. And beneath the fear rode a certainty and excitement.

When they reached the ship's side, Caleb called up, "Hello! We are here to join you!"

Then there was shouting, and a moment later musket fire from overhead, aiming at the little boat. The musket ball struck the water two feet from Caleb and Galen.

"Missed!" said a voice from above.

Caleb and Galen cowered, then Caleb shouted, "We want to join with you to subdue the rebels! Don't shoot us!"

Caleb could make out the silhouettes of more men on board above them, pointing the barrels of muskets in their direction. "Try again!" came another voice. "Spies down there, I'll venture!"

Galen whispered, "What have we done? We are in trouble here!"

"We're runaways!" called Caleb. "We saw the notice Lord Dunmore issued! Please let us aboard!"

A lantern was held over the side and Caleb was blinded in its sudden light. "Ah, slaves indeed!" said one voice.

"Just what we need," said another voice, exasperated.

Galen called up, "We've come to join you!"

"Who are you?" came the demand.

Caleb could see now, on either side of the ship's ladder, open canon hatches from which the mighty guns stared out with their single, giant eyes. He took a deep breath and said, "Negroes from Maryland, seeking to fight for England and our liberty! We heard of Dunmore's proclamation to slaves and servants. Let us on board, please sirs!"

There was a pause, then a voice hollered, "He made the proclamation more than six months ago! We got more bleedin' Negroes than we know what to do with, molderin' in our ships! Coughing out their lungs and dreaming of glory!"

"Let 'em up," said another voice. "Dunmore wants all he can get." Then, to Caleb and Galen, "Come up, then, and quickly, before I change my mind and decide you are spies and kick ye off.

There be sharks in those waters who'd love a taste of yer flesh."

Caleb pulled himself out of the boat and up the slippery rungs of the ship-side ladder, with Galen close behind. They swung their legs over the railing and dropped to the deck.

It was hard to see clearly. There were only four lanterns, one held by the sailor on a post near the front of the ship and two by a huge wheel on a raised platform at the rear. Caleb couldn't tell how many sailors were aboard, but it felt like a thousand eyes were on him. Beneath his feet, the ship shifted back and forth.

"Got no belongings?" asked one sailor, snatching at Caleb's shirt. "Bloody trouble, having no belongings for us to go through!"

The sailors laughed. One said, "Slaves always the same, mate. Have nothing but the shirts on their backs!"

"Though," said a third sailor, "I do say I've seen some of 'em fight with more determination than some of our lot. The battle at Great Bridge proved to me they got the soul for weapons and war."

"Curses!" said yet another sailor in the darkness. "Don't say things to swell their heads!"

"What you staring at?" asked the first sailor. "You show respect to the sailors of Dunmore's flotilla!"

Caleb found himself looking at the deck. "Yes, sir."

"Well, down the hatch, the both of you!" said the sailor. "And keep yer bleedin' hands to yerself. Don't be touchin' anything you know nothin' of, or we'll put you through the gauntlet before yer first night is over."

Caleb and Galen squinted, trying to see where they were supposed to go.

"The hatch!" shouted the sailor, and he gave both Caleb and Galen a shove. They stumbled forward, and found themselves teetering on the brink of a large square hole in floor. "That's right, boys!" There was more laughter.

Caleb and Galen climbed through the hole, down a steep set of steps, and dropped onto the deck below. Squinting hard to see in the light of a single lantern by the steps, Caleb could see canons by the walls, their noses poking out through holes in the walls, and among the canons, hammocks strung like drying peapods. In the hammocks were snoring, dozing sailors. From above, the sailors shouted, "Not that deck! That's for regular sailors! You got another to go!"

Feeling their way along between hammocks and the huge canons, their wheels set in blocks at the portholes, Caleb and Galen sought the hatch to the next deck. They moved carefully so as not to disturb the dozing sailors. Caleb reached out and ran his hand along a canon. It was cold and solid, and the smell was that of smoke and powder.

What battles have these mighty guns seen? Caleb wondered. *What fights have they won against slave owners?*

There were small rooms with locked doors throughout the otherwise huge deck. What were in them? Caleb couldn't know. He knew nothing of ships. He fought down a growing sense of uncertainty as the ship groaned and complained around him.

They found the hatch to the deck below, more with their feet than eyes, and eased themselves down the steep steps into the darker darkness, the coughing, and the stench.

There are sick men here, Caleb knew immediately.

Have we been sent to stay with the sick men on this ship?
He ran his hand across his eyes, and felt a shiver
cross his spine.

"Where do we go?" whispered Galen. "Where do
we sleep?"

"I don't know," said Caleb. "Any place there is
room."

The two felt their way not far from the steps and
curled up beside several barrels. Caleb stared into
the darkness, trying to get his bearings, but it was
impossible. He would have to wait until morning
to see what they had gotten themselves into.

And he prayed things would seem better in light
of day.

Caleb's sleep was shattered by a sharp poking to
his ribs, and a hearty chuckle from over his head.
He opened his eyes to what he thought was the
sun, but then saw it was a lantern, being held by
a pair of black fingers.

"Look! We took on some driftwood during the
night!"

Caleb blinked. Beside him, Galen was startled
awake, and sat up, rubbing his eyes.

The man holding the lantern was a very tall,
bald black man in a long, unbleached linen shirt
and no trousers. He had a grin that showed as
many teeth as a bear. He held out his empty hand,
and in turn, Caleb and Galen shook it. "Didn't
hear the watch bell ring, did you?" he said. "Ah,
you'll come to hear it! Welcome to the orlop deck
of the frigate *Emma!* Name's Ammiel. Ammiel Liberty, as of seven months ago. Run off from my
master in Williamsburg, where I was a house servant. I fight with the King's men now. Fighting
with the Ethiopian Regiment. Got a battle scar al-

ready, at Great Bridge. What a battle it was, with the blacks of the Regiment in the front, leading with our arms and swords!"

"Ah, close your mouth, Ammiel," grumbled another man somewhere nearby. "We lost the battle. My best friend was killed. There was nothing there but death and blood."

"I'm talking here, Joseph," said Ammiel over his shoulder. He turned back to Caleb. "Great Bridge was the battle, and we may have lost but we gave 'em a scare! We had our regiment slogan on our shirts, 'Liberty to Slaves,' and then didn't we see, face-to-face, that we were fighting a battalion of Virginians wearing 'Liberty or Death' on their own shirts! Had I not been shot then in the side, I might have laughed. We were both fighting for liberty, yet there we were, firing at each other! God must shake His great head at such a thing."

Ammiel held up his shirt, and there, indeed, was a sunken spot in his side where a musket ball had pierced through.

"I see," said Caleb.

"A wound I wear proudly," said Ammiel. "God save the King! And who are you?"

"Caleb Jacobson. I was a horse handler in Maryland."

"Fine, fine, but no need for that on board the *Emma!*" said Ammiel. "What's wrong with your hand?"

"My mother was frightened by a hawk when she was carrying me."

"Ah," said Ammiel. "And what of your quiet friend?"

"I'm Galen Stone," said Galen. "I was a barn cleaner, a fence mender, and a road builder."

"Yes!" said Ammiel. "There's an asset! We dig

many holes and mend many fences in the Regiment. You both healthy?"

Caleb and Galen nodded. Caleb looked around now, stretching out the kinks they'd gained in the night, to where men of various ages, sizes, skin colors, and degrees of health were struggling from sleep in lantern light. Unlike the sailors on the deck above, none of these had hammocks. They lay on thin blankets, and a few had mattresses. Some, who seemed isolated in a far corner where the light was most dim, were not getting up at all. Occasionally one would lean on an elbow and cough phlegm into a bucket. Besides the men, there were barrels and crates on this deck, rolls of canvas, and another hatch, to some deeper, darker deck Caleb imagined.

"Some of us got the smallpox," he said with a sigh. "No room in the sick bay where the white folks go when they're ill. Our ship isn't as bad off as some of the others in the fleet, but it's getting 'round."

"Smallpox!" said Galen.

"Just don't get too close to them," said Ammiel. "I've not got it. Maybe you won't, either, God willing."

"God willing," said Caleb earnestly.

"First thing," said Ammiel, reaching into a sack and drawing out a razor. "Got to shave your heads. Don't worry, you won't stay like me, yours'll grow back." He rubbed his head with his free hand. "Been this way since I was twenty!"

"Why you have to shave us?" asked Galen.

"Cause if I don't, the surgeon will, and he shaves not so carefully. Seen lots of bloody nicks on scalps."

"But why?" asked Caleb.

"Don't want no lice on board."

"Don't have lice," said Galen.

"Do or don't, still need shavin'," said Ammiel.

Other men got to their feet and slipped into trousers, shoes, jackets. Caleb and Galen sat still as Ammiel scraped their hair from their heads, then they stood and put on their shoes.

Caleb noticed that the air on the orlop deck not only smelled, but it was damp as if it had rained inside. Caleb's shoes were uncomfortably moist, as was his skin, and everything around him. It made him itchy.

"We got extra shirts, breeches, and waistcoats," said Ammiel. "Couple men died 'bout your size." He went to a crate, and rummaged through, then pulled out two dirty white shirts, with embroidered slogans stitched boldly across the breast. "Liberty to Slaves." Then he handed Caleb and Galen two pairs of stiff breeches and foul-smelling coats with brass buttons and scrolled cuffs. "Will find you a spoon, cup, and plate at mealtime. You won't much like what you put in the plate, but it's better than eating off the deck."

"When do we get arms?" asked Galen as he and Caleb dressed. "I'm ready to fight!"

"When we have the time and place," said Ammiel.

"What do we do until then?" asked Caleb.

Ammiel laughed. "You'll be given duties. Each time we take on new Negroes, Corporal decides what they are to do. Clean cannon balls, repair ropes, caulk decks. Haul the dead up to be sewn in canvas and dropped overboard."

Galen looked indignant. "Cleaning cannon balls? What of setting sail to meet our enemy?"

All around deck, more lanterns had been lit,

and more black men were dressed in their Ethiopian Regiment uniforms with the embroidered shirts, linen trousers, stockings, and shoes. *For what?* Caleb thought. *Spreading pitch?*

Ammiel said, "We been sitting here at the mouth of the Elizabeth River for many months. Some since last summer. Dunmore, who was Virginia's royal governor in Williamsburg, couldn't stay because most of the citizens grew very angry the way he locked up the magazine and kept arms from them. He left, and boarded his ship, aptly named *Dunmore,* and has been living there ever since. Even had his family with him before he sent 'em on to England. There have been battles, oh yes, Great Bridge in December, and then Norfolk in January. The entire city burned, you know, gone in just a few days! But mostly we've been on our ships, bobbin' on the waves, taking on citizens loyal to the king, members of the King's army, escaped slaves, the like."

"Call ourselves the 'floating town,' " said Joseph, who Caleb could see more clearly now as he'd lit his lantern. This man was medium-height, and wore a beard and a scar over his right eye. "Got over a hundred ships in this fleet."

Ammiel nodded. "We get sniped at by colonists on the shore. We snipe at them. For a long while, there were loyalists who lived along the shore who sent us supplies—food, medicines, ammunition. But just a few weeks ago, Major General Charles Lee, who commands the Southern Department of the Continental Army, ordered a complete evacuation of the harbor of Hampton Roads, the water in which we now rest. That way, there are no civilians to send us supplies."

"We came through an empty town," said Galen.

"Only soldiers there, no citizens we could see."

"And the evacuation's working," coughed another man, this one lying against a wall on a mattress with his knees drawn up and sweat dotting his forehead. His skin was covered with raised spots. Smallpox. "We eatin' once a day now. Find yourself a rat, boys, whack 'em and stuff him in your shirt. Make a good dinner."

Caleb didn't know what to say. This was a British ship, set for battle. And men had little food or ammunition? That was not the way it was supposed to be.

"Come on with us," said Ammiel, patting Caleb and Galen on the shoulders. The men who were well were already moving up the steep stairs to the deck above. "Up the companionway with you! It's four in the morning! Day has begun!"

22

ACCORDING TO AMMIEL'S explanation as the men climbed to the gun deck and then the main deck, every man on board had to make account for himself on the main deck after the second watch. The second watch began at midnight and ended at four. It didn't matter that only the seamen took part in the watch as they were trained in the finer workings of the ship. Every able-bodied soul, be he a member of the Ethiopian Regiment, the 14th Regiment, the Queen's Own Loyal Virginians, or the Royal Navy, had to be up and at attention to begin the day properly. The civilian loyalists on board, and there were about twelve of them in various cabins, were allowed to sleep until sunrise.

It was dark as night, with not even a hint of sun over the water to the east. Caleb and Galen stood in line on the main deck with the others as a grumbling lieutenant in a red jacket with white cross belts gave a cursory check of the sailors and soldiers. The white men stood at the front and the

Ethiopian Regiment stood at the back. There was a breeze off the bay, cool and salty, and Caleb took deep breaths to try to wake himself completely. It would not do to be less than alert on his very first day on board.

After what was a nearly incoherent and fierce rambling about duty, honor, the continued pressure from shore by the bloody colonial rebels, rats in the hold, the spreading smallpox on the orlop deck, and the anticipation of reinforcement from Royal Navy Captain Andrew Hammond, to which Dunmore had sent an appeal just days earlier, the lieutenant dismissed the men to their chores about the ship.

Ammiel took Caleb and Galen back down to the orlop deck with most of the other Ethiopians.

"Spoke with Corporal Richman," he said as they reached the bottom of the steps. "He wants you in the bread room, sucking maggots from the biscuits."

"Indeed?" asked Caleb. Had he heard correctly?

"Bread room's down the other end of the deck, port side, past the sick men, the carpenter's store, and the pump shaft," said Ammiel. "The steward's mate is there and will tell you what to do." He chuckled. "Steward's mate can't tolerate working down here now, what with the smallpox. Watch out for him, he's got a temper and a stick!"

Caleb nodded. Galen said, "What's your duty?"

"Ah," said Ammiel. "Varies. This morning I help the steward draw rations from the store and take them up to the sailor's cooks, for the crew and the civilian breakfast."

And when will we eat? My stomach is waging war with me at this moment! Caleb wondered, but knew it was not time to ask. They would learn more by watching than by speaking.

The bread room was a long but narrow closet in which sacks of biscuits were stored for the entire population of the ship. The biscuits were different from any Caleb had seen before; these were hard as stones and, on close inspection, crawling with maggots. Inside the room was a short, bushy white man in uniform trousers and shirt and a greasy scarf wrapped about his neck. He was hanging a lantern on a wall hook, and wiping his forehead with the heel of his hand. Leaning against the wall was a huge stick.

"New, are you?" he demanded. "I see those bald heads! I'm the steward's mate, and it's my duty to look after the store, be it bread or peas or cheese. I measure 'em out for the steward, and I measure well, don't think I don't! Some ships got steward's mates who steal food, and sell it to seamen for shillings on the side. I never done that!"

"I didn't think you did," said Caleb.

"Talk when you're asked to talk!" said the steward's mate. "You ain't sick, are ye?"

"I don't think so," said Galen.

"Hate being down here with them sick boys," grumbled the steward's mate. "Now, we got lots of creatures sharing our provisions. Rats. Maggots. Weevils. Oh, we all eat 'em at times, can't be helped, and a black-headed maggot ain't so bitter on the tongue, not like them weevils. But we got to clean up the biscuits best we can. Suck out the maggots."

Caleb and Galen nodded.

"Bag of fish is on its way from atop," continued the steward's mate. "What you do is this; lay a dead fish atop all the biscuit sacks. Maggots'll crawl out the biscuits and into the fish 'cause they like to eat fish better'n bread. When the fish is full of maggots, put it in a bucket and put another atop the sack. Gets most the maggots out the biscuits that way. When all the sacks been done, take the buckets of fish atop and throw 'em into the bay."

Caleb said, "Yes, sir."

Galen said, "Yes, sir."

The steward tipped his head at the stick and said, "While waitin' on the worms you go after the rats."

A minute later, several men handed four heavy sacks of newly-caught fish through the door. Some were still alive, and wriggled against their situation. Caleb and Galen each took out a fish, opened biscuit sacks, and lay the fish on top of the bread. Then, they went down the line, putting fish in each opened sack. Caleb knew this was a job that could take most of the day, but he didn't mind. He was with the British Navy. He was doing his part.

I just have to be patient, he thought, *and look further than this moment to see the brighter future.* Then Caleb paused, and tipped his head, knowing he'd heard something like that before. But where? And from whom?

Mealtime for the Ethiopian Regiment came at noon, and all the black men gathered on their deck to eat what had been cooked by one of their fellows. Ammiel sat on the floor beside Caleb and Galen, munching his biscuit—which had only one maggot—and piece of salt pork, and explaining the differences between the white crews and the blacks.

"We eat cold foods down here," he said. "We don't have a place to cook anything. Up on the gun deck, the sailors got tables they pull down and sit at. They eat three times a day, we eat once."

"You tryin' to stir up a mutiny over there, Ammiel?" said Joseph, who was seated near a barrel, and had a mouthful of biscuit and ale.

"Just jawin'," said Ammiel. "Tellin' our new friends the way of the world." He looked back at Caleb and Galen. "*Emma*'s got fifty-four cannons, twenty four-pounders on the main deck and thirty two-pounders on the gun deck. Captain and First Lieutenant sleep in cabins on the quarterdeck atop. On the gun deck there's lodgings for the junior lieutenant and chaplain, the purser, surgeon, gunner, and carpenter. The civilians sleep where they can, some with the sailors on hammocks and most in the cabins."

"When do we fight?" Galen asked.

"You a hot-headed man, ain't cha?" said Ammiel. "I told you. When the time comes. Not 'til then."

The afternoon was long and hot, with Caleb and Galen back in the bread room, tossing maggot-filled fish into buckets and killing rats. Caleb had not seen the light of day since the day before, and longed for just a glimpse of the sun. It was with a sense of relief and anticipation that he and Galen at last were given leave to take the first of the worm-riddled fish to the main deck to throw overboard.

The sunlight was bright, nearly blinding, and Caleb had to pause for a moment to catch his breath and his balance. He felt light-headed and woozy, and wondered if it was the onset of smallpox or just an unfamiliarity with the constant rocking of the ship. The sky was near-white, and circling it were large white birds with black-tipped wings. They soared and swooped, diving for fish at the surface of the water.

The sight of the main deck in daylight hours as opposed to the pitch-black hours of night was amazing, indeed. Sailors were all about, from deck to highest point on the masts, cleaning, repairing, checking, watching. There was a small unit of men practicing with their swords, sparring with each other with jabs and flicks. Other sailors were on hands and knees, scrubbing the wooden floor. Some of the men were washing hammocks and clothing in wooden tubs, while yet others sat with a huge sail draped over their knees, sewing up places that had been clearly rubbed apart against the ropes. One man was tied to a far mast, and several others, petty officers Caleb guessed, were going at him with an unraveled length of rope. The man cried with each blow, and Caleb looked away.

Several small boats were tied to this deck and covered with canvas. On a section of deck higher than that of the main deck, a man with a large hat and long tube was staring out across the water in all directions. Near this man were several men and women, trying to appear contained and dignified in their civilian clothing, but their weather-worn faces and squinting eyes revealing the wear of a long time on board.

"This *is* a floating town," said Galen as he and Caleb took the buckets to the side of the ship and flung the contents out onto the waves. "Just look about. Ships as far as you can see. We're part of a town, Caleb, and God knows we never have to go back!"

From the vantage point on the deck of the *Emma*, Caleb could see many of the other ships that were part of the flotilla. All sizes they were, from small, flat ships with only one mast and no guns to huge ships with four masts and what seemed to be three gun decks. It was hard to see beyond the ships, or to see much on the shores of the Elizabeth River or across the wide stretch of Hampton Roads. Caleb knew the man with the looking-tube was watching for snipers. It was what he would do if he was in charge of this ship.

Caleb and Galen took five trips, hauling up the rest of the maggoty fish to dump in the bay. Caleb kept his ears open, knowing that as a simple, black soldier he wouldn't be told directly what was happening until it filtered down through the ranks. He tried to piece together snippets of conversation he heard from passing seamen and officers, so that his new life would make more sense.

"The lieutenant of the hospital brig *Adonis* called over. They've lost another nine in their beds. Seven of smallpox. Two of a fever."

"There were shots fired at us from Craney Island. Second watch fired back. Lasted only twenty minutes, then all went still."

"Dunmore still awaits word that reinforcement will come. Is he hoping to receive help to bombard the shores here, or shall we move elsewhere? There is nothing for us here now but emptying stores and water growing stale. I pray we leave. I have grown to hate those ragged lines of land as much as the persistent insurgents who populate them!"

The days that followed fell into a routine. Rising at the bell at the end of second watch at four o'clock, laboring until the mid-day meal, then laboring again until it was time to sleep at the beginning of the first watch at eight. Caleb and

Galen were given a variety of the most humble jobs, as were most of the Ethiopian Regiment; decked out in their embroidered shirts they broke empty barrels into fuel wood and hauled it to the galley stove for the white men's hot meals, they sewed torn uniforms, killed rats, and checked endless feet of deck planks for cracks which they then caulked with rope fibers and sealed with pitch.

There were members of the Ethiopian Regiment on other ships, Caleb and Galen learned, likely doing the same as they to keep the stationary flotilla from falling to complete disrepair and vermin infestation. Caleb thought how fine it would be, to have an Ethiopian ship to themselves. But although Dunmore had given arms to the black men on shore and had trained them for battle, it was clear the other officers didn't have the same trust or respect. Perhaps they would be afraid that with a ship of their own, the Ethiopian Regiment would run amok and be lost at sea.

Perhaps we would find a battle and win it instead of rotting here, Caleb thought glumly.

Sometimes at night, after the bell rang for the beginning of first watch, some of the black soldiers would, with a few coins of their wages, bribe the sailors on the gun deck, and be allowed to fish from the open gun ports. Through these holes the men lowered hooks baited with maggots into the sea, and prayed they would draw them back up with a catch. Then, with a bucket and bit of flint and wood chips, a fish could be cooked to some degree of edibility when everyone but second watch had gone to sleep.

One evening, on his way down to the orlop deck after first watch bell, Caleb noticed a sailor on the floor by his hammock, struggling to read a letter by lantern light. He hesitated, then went to the man and said, "If you will let me fish from a port tonight, I shall read your letter to you. You seem to be having trouble."

The man was furious. "I can read it!" he said. "You impertinent fool! Get back from me! Of course I can read. Lighting's bad is all! Away with ye!"

The other sailors, climbing into their hammocks amid the cannons, chuckled at the fury in their friend's voice.

"You tell 'em, Samuel!" said one.

But the following evening, after a long day of caulking the main deck in the rain, Caleb was stopped on his way down the steps by Samuel, who spoke quickly and so no one else could hear him. "Come up to the gun deck tonight. You'll read me the letter. Let no one see you, hear me?"

And so it was that after an hour had elapsed, Caleb sneaked up the companionway to Samuel's deck, and the two hid behind the wall to the surgeon's cabin. All about the deck, the men in hammocks snored soundly, and the ship creaked incessantly. Caleb held up a candle he'd brought from his supplies, and read Samuel's letter in a whisper.

It was from his wife, and had been written seven months earlier. She lived in London, and spoke of the farm, the children, and her ailing mother. Samuel listened intently, his hands clasped in his lap, his head tilted to catch every word. When Caleb was done, the man said quietly, "I've had that letter since February. It is all I have of my family."

Caleb nodded. He had nothing of his family.

"You read well for a Negro. How is that so?"

"I was raised with Quakers. They believe in equality of the races, be they Negro or white. I went to school."

"Mmm," said Samuel. Then he said, "You write as well as you read?"

"Yes."

Samuel scratched his chin. "It is not that I can't read or write. I can. I read that letter many a time. But . . ." He stopped. He stared into the dark space of the gun deck. "My eyes. My eyes are failing me. I can't have no one find out, ye hear? If they know, there will be no more Navy for me."

Caleb nodded again.

Then Samuel grabbed Caleb's shirt and drew his face close to his own. "You'll say nothing of this, you hear me? Or I'll accuse you of mutiny, and they'll have you flogged around the fleet for it, they will! They'll tie you to a capstan and whip you on your back about the whole of the fleet, around every ship we have. Most men die from it!"

"I'll say nothing," said Caleb.

Then Samuel went silent. Caleb said, "Would you like me to write a letter for you? Is there means to send it to England? Have you pen and ink?"

Samuel chewed on a loose piece of fingernail, then spat it out. "No way to send a letter now," he said. "But I would like to write one. One I can send when times are better. You write one for me and I'll give you a go at a porthole to draw all the fish you can eat. Ye deem that a fair trade?"

"I'd rather have paper, pen, and ink myself," said Caleb. "I can survive on dried peas and biscuits, but I long to write of where I am."

"Ah, ye make a hard bargain!" swore Samuel. But he shook his head then, and said, "I'll have the paper, pen, and ink. And ye shall write for me whenever I need. Whenever, I say. Do you understand me?"

"Yes," said Caleb. "Thank you, sir."

Samuel threw up a hand. "Don't thank me. Just get back down to your deck 'fore anyone sees me talking to you!"

23

May 13, 1776

I feel as if the whole of Dunmore's fleet is holding its breath, waiting. Galen and I have been on board for not three full weeks, yet we are anxious and growing well weary of life on the Emma with no sign of battle. The only sights we see are the other ships, the far shores of the Elizabeth River, and each other. As much as Galen and Ammiel and Joseph are my friends, I do tire of their constant visage.

Every few nights, Samuel has me write a short missive to his wife. He knows she will not receive them until the fighting between England and the Americans is over, or until he is killed in battle. He puts them into his haversack. He insists I let no one know that I write for him. He does not want his shipmates to know of his failing eyesight, but I believe he does not want some of his white mates to know that a Negro can write and read when some of them cannot.

Curses! My body aches for fairness!

I was afflicted with the sea sickness for two days, and was unable to eat even a handful of cheese.

Ammiel said it happened to most men when they were not used to being on the sea. I thought I should die. I tried my best to work, but my bowels forced me to spend much time with my head over a bucket, or hanging over the side of the main deck. I am well now, and pray to God I will never have sea sickness again.

Benjamin Banneker said I should write him when I arrived at my destination. I could not send a letter to him if I wanted to, as there are no shipments going on or off the Emma, or any other ship as far as I can see. Boats that try to make it to us, or boats that would try to make it to shore are shot at by the soldiers of the colonies. There are Continental cannons trained on us, with more being put into position near the mouth of the river. Who knows how long until a full-fledged attack comes upon us? So as it is, I could not write a letter to Mr. Banneker if I wanted to, as he would not receive it.

Although I have no desire to write the gentleman. His words offended me.

I have yet to see Lord Dunmore, the man for whom we have come to fight. I can see the flag on his ship when I am on the main deck, but that flag is silent. What are his thoughts? What are his plans?

This morning another of the Ethiopian Regiment, a fellow named Percy, perished of the smallpox. With God's grace neither Ammiel, Galen, nor I have succumbed to this wicked disease. The steward's mate has, however, and has taken to his hammock. He was replaced with a mute boy, a sailor, who does his job without complaint.

It fell to Galen and myself to wrap Percy in his blanket and haul him up to the sail maker. The man was fairly light, as his body was shrunk down to naught but skin and bones. I thought as I was carrying him, here, God, is another of your black sons, *being made to go where he did not choose to go. Where he did not want to go.*

But if we could only fight! Bring me a slave owner and a pistol and let us have at our destinies!

❧ 24 ❧

WE SAIL IN a week's time!" came the urgent mutterings of the sailors and soldiers as they mustered on the main deck for the four o'clock count. The morning was muggy and hot already, with the air so heavy with salt that Caleb had struggled with dressing as his clothes stuck and clung to his body like barnacles on the bottom of the ship.

"Praise God we're going to leave!" said one.

"I've heard New York," said another.

"I've heard Yorktown," said a third.

"Quit yammerin'," said Ammiel, "we'll hear the truth in but a moment if you'll just close your mouths!"

"I don't care where we go," said Galen as he and Caleb reached the top of the companionway and stepped onto the main deck. "As long as we are given our arms and training. Ammiel wears his wound from Great Bridge with pride. I don't wear my lash marks with anything but shame. I want something I can be proud of."

The crews moved into place in line, waiting for Lieutenant Richardson to arrive for his morning talk. It took a good ten minutes longer than usual, and the men stood silently, eyeing each other and awaiting the good word.

The captain of the ship, Abraham Monte, came out with the lieutenant and stood before the men. Caleb had rarely seen the captain, had only had rare glimpses of the man as he'd strolled about the quarterdeck and main deck, the brim of his huge feathered hat obscuring his face.

Captain Monte cleared his throat and said, "Good morning, men. We've news from Lord Dunmore."

There was a barely audible shifting among the men of the crews, and Caleb knew that every one of them was as anxious to get something done as he was.

"Captain Andrew Hammond and his fleet anchored near us yesterday, as you are all aware. The Captain spent many hours with Lord Dunmore, in order to determine the best course of action for our fair ships and stalwart men. The word is thus— we are to make needed repairs on all ships. We are to evacuate those which are not seaworthy and take onto those that are able to sail all crew members and passengers. We will relocate to Gwynn's Island. Hammond has seen this bit of land, and assures Lord Dunmore that it is an excellent site from which to carry on our military campaign. There is a defensible shore there, water, provisions, and deep anchorage. The population of the island is moderate, many of whom are sympathizers with the rebels, but they will not expect us, and we should have no trouble establishing ourselves there."

There broke out cheering then, and neither Caleb nor Galen could stop themselves from cheering, too. Hats were tossed in the air, and men clapped their hands in joy. Some swung each other around by the elbows.

Lieutenant Richardson lifted his sword, demanding the men be at order immediately, but Captain Monte put his hand on the shoulder of his officer and shook his head. He would allow the moment of celebration.

The following days were full of flurry. Ropes were repaired, sails stitched cleanly, and the outsides of the ships scoured by sailors who dangled on ropes from the main deck. Although Caleb and Galen were given the tedious chore of cleaning cannonballs in the shot locker, coating each heavy shot with a good layer of grease to remove the rust, they didn't complain. Even though the shot locker was in the hold, the lowest, filthiest, and smelliest deck on the ship, neither questioned their assignment. These were the shots that would be used in the fight for freedom and justice, and they deserved to be cleaned well and made ready for the guns. When done, they took several crates full up to the gun deck, where the six-man gun crew was drilling with the cannons. Caleb watched for a moment as the men cleaned, loaded, aimed, and fired the great guns into the water. He knew he could do it. All he needed was a chance.

The *Emma* took on twenty-three new citizens from one of the smaller sloops, which was in such dire condition that it would be destroyed by its own crew before the fleet went north up the Chesapeake Bay. The citizens were sea-weary and grumpy, but seemingly glad to be aboard a vessel which had a chance of staying afloat. Several more boatloads of loyalists, including some wives of the Ethiopian Regiment, were shipped from Tucker's Point on the coast to the floating town under the protection of Hammond's pilot ships.

Ammiel made comment while scrubbing down his shirt in a bucket of brackish water one night that if he'd had a wife, he wouldn't want her amid the men sick with smallpox. "I'd have her on another ship before I'd have her here," he said, almost angrily, looking over at the three women who had become part of the citizenship on the orlop deck. The women, also escaped slaves who had been hiding at Tucker's Point with loyalist families, seemed tough enough to withstand whatever the sailing north might incur. They were stout women with strong arms and determined faces. Yet even the strongest, most determined man could fall victim to the pox.

"How come you don't got a wife?" asked Galen. He was sitting in a wooden tub, scrubbing himself from head to toe in water that had seen the baths of the previous seven men. The water was gray and had a skim of lime soap.

Ammiel rubbed his hand over his bald head. "Did," he said. "Died in childbirth. She was a cook where I was a house servant. A beautiful woman, tall, slender, fingers that could make the most delicate basket or cook the most wonderful-smelling pork roast. Our first child it would've been."

"Where's your child?" asked Caleb.

"Dead, too," said Ammiel. "Master's little boy was playing with her. She was two. Swung her around, he did, and smacked her head 'gainst a fence post. Broke her neck."

Caleb caught his breath. "I'm sorry," he said.

"She woulda been seven this summer. August

19th. Little Sophie." Ammiel shook his head as if to clear it, then said, "And you boys? Any wives among you two?"

"Was a girl I liked at River's Pine, called Jewel," said Galen. "Liked her 'bout ten months, and woulda married her 'cept Master got her in the family way then sold her off for twice the price. After that, I decided I wouldn't fall in love. Too much hurtin' in love. Too much loss."

"And you, Caleb?" asked Ammiel. "You was a free boy, yes? Did you have a woman before you come down here? Free man's got a lot to offer a woman."

"I'm sixteen," said Caleb.

"I loved my first woman at fourteen," said Ammiel.

"There was a girl once," Caleb said, "but didn't matter I was free or slave. Her father said I could never see her again." Caleb was stunned to see Charity's face in his mind, her sweet smile and gentle eyes. He had tried his best to forget everything about Quality and Quantity, and had done a fair job of it. But for that moment, he thought of her, and felt himself go quiet and sullen at the loss.

He slept fitfully that night, though he had slept a good twenty-eight nights aboard the *Emma* and had come to know well it's groans, smells, and motions. His dreams were but vicious and painful images. Charity and Jeremiah Martin saying vows as she wept. Francis Jacobson being chased by a four-legged, wolflike Mr. Whitley through a dense Maryland forest. Caleb himself jumping into the cold water of the East River as the man he'd always thought of as his father stood on shore and shouted, "You are no hero, you paddle-paw! You can't save anyone, not even yourself!"

The second watch bell cut his dream, and he was glad, this once, to be up at four o'clock with duties to perform.

And duties there were. The day was May 26th, and it was a Sunday, so after the ship's chaplain stood in the fog and gave an early, two-hour sermon on God's divine plan for the Christian nation of England and it's holy destiny to crews and citizens alike on the main deck, it was time to set sail up the Chesapeake Bay to Gwynn's Island a good thirty nautical miles away. "We beseech thee Lord to still the waters and lead thy children safely upon thy hand," the chaplain prayed, "to the place thou will have us be. In the name of our Savior the Lord Jesus Christ, Amen."

The gathering echoed "Amen." And then Captain Monte, who stood above the rest on the quarterdeck, his hat feather blowing in the wind, raised his hand. Then he cried, "Let fall!" Seamen went to work. Sails were unfurled and snapped at the air like giant white dogs, while the men on the yard held on skillfully so as not to be knocked from the rigging. Everywhere Caleb could see, as he turned complete circles on the deck, the other ships were unfurling sails and tying them in place. And the ships began to move—pilot boats, sloops, snows, brigs, frigates, man-of-wars. With Captain Hammond's *Roebuck* in the lead, the ships moved into position so as not to bottleneck the mouth of the river and to make it safely through Hampton Roads and to the mighty bay. There were men manning the cannons below, for there might be a last-effort attack by Colonial militia, hidden somewhere in the lush summer growth along the shores.

But no attack came. Obviously the fleet was so impressive it kept the rebels silent.

The fog burned away by seven, and by noon all the ships were in the bay. The wind was kind, blowing from the southwest. Caleb and Galen, wanting to watch the progress of the fleet, found work on the main deck swabbing the floors with large blocks of stone which the sailors called "holystones" because they were as large and heavy as family Bibles. On their knees they moved about the deck, staying clear of the scurrying feet of the sailors. It was a fine day to be in the sun and the breezes. Caleb found himself smiling openly. Even Galen, who had stripped from his jacket and shirt, exposing his scarred back, was able to laugh when he saw a clumsy sailor slip, hit his backside, and bounce like a ball on the wet deck.

The trip was uneventful and short. By late afternoon the fleet was in sight of the island, which sat to the left of the bay and was separated by the mainland by a channel and deep river. The *Roebuck* anchored at the northern tip of the island, keeping watch as all the other ships moved into the river. By nightfall all the ships were anchored safely.

The Ethiopian Regiment went to bed reluctantly that evening. Amid the moans of the sick and the chewing of the rats in and behind the barrels on the orlop deck, the men sat on their mattresses and predicted what would face them when the sun came up again. Ammiel thought they would be immediately attacked by the locals on the island. Another man said the locals would be so fearful of the mighty fleet, they would be long gone by the time morning arrived.

Caleb didn't know. And it didn't matter. He wrote:

God bless Lord Dunmore and Captain Hammond. The might of the British Navy is beyond any I have seen. Their might and wisdom is ordained by God, so says the chaplain. And I believe him. I do believe him!

❧ 25 ❧

THE ISLAND SOIL was a welcomed sensation beneath Caleb's feet. As he hopped from the small boat onto the shore he felt for a moment that he would lose his balance for the stillness of the earth. But then he regained himself, and followed the rest of the Ethiopian Regiment and the Queen's Own Loyal Virginians up the slope of the waterside bank. All around him were soldiers in uniform. The Virginians in their gold-trimmed jackets, buckskin breeches, and tall boots. The Ethiopians in their jackets with brass buttons, short boots, leather leggings, and their embroidered "Liberty to Slaves" shirts.

It was just after sunrise. At four that morning, Hammond's marines had explored the shoreline in small boats. Now, it was time to determine what was on the island. Dunmore had put that task to the Virginians and Ethiopian.

Ammiel was in charge of the *Emma*'s Ethiopian battalion, which Caleb and Galen discovered that morning was actually a smaller group than on the other ships, for once the whole of the Regiment—seven battalions in all—had disembarked and mustered on the island, Caleb saw that they consisted of at least two hundred men, possibly more.

Caleb found himself standing amid black men of all ages and sizes, standing straight and alert, dressed in uniform, and, as Galen had been wanting since they first boarded the *Emma* back in late April, bearing Brown Bess flintlock muskets with bayonets, and pouches with cartridges containing lead balls and pre-measured gunpowder.

A Sergeant Culpepper of the Queen's Own ordered his men to march the southern length of the island. Sergeant Freeman, who was the highest ranking Ethiopian officer since the battle at Great Bridge, immediately took charge of the Ethiopian battalions. He raised his voice and said, "We take the northern length! Steady, in order now, watching for colonial militia and taking care with citizens!"

In long lines of men, thirty across and seven deep, the Ethiopians began their march across the island. Only several yards into the march, Galen whispered to Caleb, "I've got my sidearm, but don't know how to use it any more than I could read a book! I should have been shown this long ago, on the *Emma*, but no, I had maggots to lure out of biscuits!"

Caleb shook his head. "Shh," he said. "If I find the chance I'll show you. If not, I know we will drill on our return to the riverside."

"And if we face a skirmish?"

"Hide behind a rock."

The march lasted two hours, one hour across to the bay, and one hour back to the western side of the island on the river. The land was fairly even, with just the smallest of rises and falls, and criss-crossed with roads and pathways, apple groves and thick forest stands. The men did not encounter rebel militia, but the island citizens were clearly unhappy about the arrival of British forces. As the regiment moved past a small, weather-worn house with a fenced garden, a little girl shouted at them from the stoop, "Go away! Go home! Leave us be!" Her mother drew her into the house quickly, but Caleb saw the ghost image of her face lingering where she had stood. A face filled with fury, anger, and fear.

Other households took much the same attitude. Men shook fists at the regiment, women raised their hands as if to shoo them away and back onto their ships. Children threw rocks or cried. They saw few slave holders that Caleb could identify, primarily communities working their own land and raising their own crops and livestock. Primarily white, yet there were several black families which peered at the wall of passing munitions from what seemed to be the windows of their own homes.

On their return to the western shore, the Ethiopians discovered that a camp was well under construction, with lines being drawn and tents being erected. A lieutenant Caleb had never seen before, named Eibert, took over command of the black soldiers, and put them to labor on the camp in order to relieve a good many of the other troops for drilling, patrolling, and going out to procure provisions from the natives as well as housing for the civilians.

Shedding jackets and draping them over branches of ragged pines, the black men went to work with picks and shovels, digging rows of trenches and building redoubts that faced the river, the north, the south, and the east. The area was large, for there were many men who would stay ashore and man this camp. The air on the island was humid and thick, and the soil of the area was heavy and damp.

Caleb's shoulders and arms were aching by mid-morning. He paused to wipe his face and slap away gnats, then glanced down the line where men like himself were wielding tools and flinging dirt. Beside him, Galen coughed and spit out a fly that had swooped into his open mouth.

"Ah! I don't know which is the most enjoyable," Galen said as he swung the pick tip down into the soil again and drew up a mound full of rock, sand, and bugs. "Diggin' holes or suckin' maggots. What do you think, Caleb?"

"I prefer the maggots," said Caleb. "Though a good round with a pick is a close second."

"Think we'll drill soon?" asked Galen.

"I don't know. I would think so."

Galen began pulling his nose. An insect had gone up it. He was having little luck with the Gwynn's Island wildlife.

They worked for another stretch in silence, with only the sounds of the drilling soldiers and the occasional song from down the trench-digging line.

Sergeant Freeman came around the length of men, bringing with him two corporals and several buckets of clean water. Caleb and Galen paused to take long, cool drinks of the sweet water. As Freeman moved on up the line, Galen asked, "Think we'll see battle soon?"

But before Caleb could open his mouth to answer, there came a shout and the sound of gunfire from across the river. All shoveling stopped, and all heads turned in unison in the direction of the sound. There could be seen men behind trees and rocks, shooting at the island.

Then in just a moment, on the heels of the first cracks of Colonial rifles, officers of the different troops were shouting orders, and commanding return fire. Sergeant Freeman called to his regiment. The Ethiopians snatched up their muskets by the trees in a quick but orderly scrambling, began adding powder and shot, then crouched behind the trenches they had been digging and aimed at the enemy on the other side of the narrow water.

Caleb expertly loaded his shot and rammed it down, then aimed the heavy gun at a flash of movement over the river. He pulled the trigger, and was dismayed at the inaccuracy of his fire. His own hunting rifle back in Maryland was much easier to aim. This British musket seemed clumsy and ill-sighted. He wished for a moment to have his own gun from home, but then remembered it was not at home but left in a sack at River's Pine. Mr. Whitley had probably hunted quite a few quail and rabbits with Caleb's rifle.

To either side, the Ethiopian Regiment was loading and firing, forming a tight and determined line along the trench. Caleb loaded his musket again, and then was grabbed by the wrist. It was Galen.

"How do I do this? I was just a slave! I can fight, I can wrestle with my hands but I don't know how to use a gun!"

"Later!" shouted Caleb. "Lay low."

"I want to fight!"

"Lay low! You have no choice!"

With a growl of anger, Galen pulled himself down into the depths of the trench amid the flashing and pounding of the muskets near him.

Just ten minutes into the fight, there was a sound of artillery, and Caleb looked north to see one of the gun ships sailing into position on the deep river, and sending cannonballs into the trees on the mainland. That was all that was needed. The Colonials withdrew, falling back into the dense growth of the shoreline forest. The sounds of gunfire echoed for a few seconds more, then faded on the air. There were cheers from the men on the island. Sergeant Freeman told his men, "They see what they are facing! We have chased them back to the woods like whipped pups!"

Word came across the camp that there had not been a single casualty, only two wounded. But the celebration was short-lived, for it was back with the picks and shovels to the trenches. By three in the afternoon, according to Joseph, who had bought a pocket watch off one of the sailors on board the *Emma* several months ago, the men were allowed to lay down their tools for a meal.

Several men, on the march across the island, had scavenged some chickens and stuck them into their jackets. Others had pulled up large handfuls of carrots and spinach, while others had spirited away plump, orange squash. Caleb hadn't noticed the thievery, but there it was, in the flesh. In the pots on the blazing fire amid the boiling peas and oatmeal that had been brought from the *Emma*, chunks of chicken, hunks of carrots, and spinach leaves floated and rolled.

Sitting on the ground with tin plates in their laps, Caleb, Galen, Ammiel, and Joseph scooped up the food and downed it in mighty mouthfuls. Aside from his mother's pork stew, Caleb couldn't remember food tasting any better.

Except, perhaps, for that which Benjamin Banneker had served them when he brought them, filthy, spent, and hungry, to his home at Ellicott Mills.

All the men, even the Ethiopian Regiment officers, licked their plates when the food was gone.

All around, the camp was taking shape. Ammunition and weapons had been brought from the ships to the land, and were being stored in a large tent. Smaller tents for the men now stood in tidy rows behind the trenches, and a hospital tent was going up in the center. Ammiel said, "Heard some of the 14th Regiment's been sent to the eastern shore to set up a quarantine camp. Get those sick men and sick civilians off the ships at last and give 'em a place away from us."

"A place to get better," said Caleb.

Ammiel scratched his scalp, then looked under his fingers as if checking for lice, although lice never fared well on a bald head. "Maybe. Or maybe to die. But it's away. It's not I don't care, but I ain't God. I can't cure 'em and neither can the doctors."

When the meal was over, it was another two hours of trench digging, then time for the Ethiopian Regiment to drill. All seven battalions went to the back of the camp, on the northeastern edge, and stood at attention while Sergeant Freeman prepared them to run through their paces. Most of these men had trained together back in late 1775, even before the Battle of Great Bridge, and they moved well and correctly to the commands as a small black boy with a drum beat the cadence.

"March!"

"Halt!"

"To the right face!"

"Halt! Front! March!"

Caleb and Galen, two of the newest volunteers, tried their best to keep up, marching, turning, passing in line, kneeling, loading their arms to fire up into the trees.

Caleb wanted to whisper instructions to Galen, but he could not. He was to be silent, as were the other men. As Galen fumbled with the flintlock on his musket and cursed quietly through his teeth, Caleb kept up with the others, and with a click of the trigger, fired neatly into the branches of an elm tree. As neatly as the musket could fire, that was. The branch he aimed for was not the branch he struck, but one decidedly to the right of it.

Suddenly, Sergeant Freedom shouted "Men to attention!" and all the regiment's men snapped up to stand straight and stare ahead. The muskets held in proper position at their sides. Galen stood by Caleb, breathing heavily, embarrassed and angry.

"Vice Admiral Dunmore, sir!" said Freeman. And out of the corner of Caleb's eye, for he could not turn or he would be out of order, he saw the man he had wondered about for so long. The man for whom he and Galen had run from Maryland, risking life and limb, the man whose vision had made it possible for slaves to be part of the noble fight.

Lord Dunmore was not tall, but stood as a man who was. He wore a dark blue coat with gold lace on the lapels, cuffs, and collar. His black hat had gold trim and tassels. His vest and breeches were white, and his scabbard and shoes matched, both of black leather. The man's hair was powdered pure white.

Sergeant Freeman said no more, for he was only a sergeant, and a Negro sergeant at that. He stared straight ahead and waited.

Lord Dunmore slowly walked the line of men, strolling with his hands behind his back. Caleb could feel the grumbling of his body as he stood still. His muscles ached for having done a long day's chopping and digging, which he'd not done in two months, and they twitched beneath his skin. *I must stand perfectly still,* Caleb thought. *It won't do for Dunmore to think I twitch from nervousness!*

Then the vice admiral came into Caleb's full view, and instead of looking straight ahead, as he knew a soldier should do, or looking down at the ground, which a Negro was expected to do in the presence of a white man, Caleb looked at Lord Dunmore. His eyes locked with the vice admiral's, and for a moment the two men, one of green eyes and one of brown, considered each other.

Dunmore tilted his head slightly, and Caleb thought he was going to smile, but the expression that spread across the man's face was of distaste and haughty superiority. His eyes narrowed in a cold threat. And in that second, the man looked like Mr. Whitley the moment he raised his crop.

Then the vice admiral was gone, down the line, strolling with his hands back and his white powdered hair reflecting the late-day sun.

The Ethiopian Regiment had tents, but the oldest and the ones with the biggest holes. Ammiel told his unit that as soon as the opportunity arose they would mend the tents, for there had been no rain in days and God wouldn't keep his finger on the spout of heaven's pump forever. Caleb shared a tent with Ammiel, Joseph, and Galen. He sat on his blanket as the other three lay with knapsacks beneath their heads to rest. He thought of the long day.

He thought of Dunmore.

And now, where no one could see him, he let his muscles do as they would. And he shook long into the night.

❧ 26 ❧

June 2, 1776

It is Sunday. The men on board the ships as well as those of us on the island held worship services under the leadership of our chaplains, praying God for continued protection from the colonials and from the weather, which, except for a gale three days ago, has been favorable. After the services, there was a reading of the articles of war to all the men in camp. Dunmore emphasized the portion on desertion, for we are close to the mainland and there is still much illness among us. Men who stay and face an enemy with a sword may run when facing an enemy of disease. The sick are taken to the quarantined camp on the eastern side of the island, but we hear there are burials daily.

The civilians on Gwynn's Island were evacuated several weeks ago, and we have free access to their homes, crops, and animals, although the officers secure most of the better foods for themselves. I felt sorry for many of the civilians, white and black, for they were not against us nor for us, only in our way. I know this is how wars are won, but I could not help but *wish that it was not so.*

*We see rebels across the river daily. They are
building fortifications in the shadows. It has been a
long time since we have been shot at, but we all know
that is because they are making their plans. We will
not be left alone much longer. They fear our numbers
and our manned ships, but they are desperate.
Desperate men do desperate things.*

Several days ago, the Spanish ship Santa Barbara
*was captured in the bay and brought to our island.
The ship claimed to be neutral and thus not subject to
capture, but there was found on the ship 12,000 pieces
of silver which, Dunmore is certain, was bound to the
Continental Congress along with an informal emissary
to the Congress from Spain. Although Captain Bellew
of the* Liverpool, *which subdued the* Santa Barbara,
*swears to have kept the chests of silver himself, I've
heard that in truth Dunmore demanded it, and in the
cloak of night has brought the chests on the island and
buried them so only he and his lieutenant know where
they are. Ah, what couldn't be had for 12,000 pieces of
silver!*

*I have thought much about Dunmore since our first
meeting. I do not like the man, but I do not have to.
His disgust with me was that of an officer for a
soldier, not a master for a slave. I will continue to do
my best for him.*

*Galen is quite a fine shot now. It took but a matter
of three days until he was missing branches in trees as
well as the rest of us.*

❧ 27 ❧

CALEB HAD SECOND watch in the wee hours of July 9th. He stood with his musket at the southern corner of the camp, watching down the shore of the river and across the water as well as the land to the east. The air from the bay was warm, salty, and humid. Caleb thought he should have been used to damp air by now, but he was not. Wet clothing, wet shoes, wet stockings, wet skin. Sticky and uncomfortable. He waved a cloud of gnats from his face and remembered the cold brisk snow that had fallen in mid-April. He remembered Nosey's sharp little hooves carving patterns in the white crust as she'd moved in circles around him on her lead.

"Stop it," he whispered to himself. "Wishing won't change a thing now. If it was cold and snowy, you'd probably be wanting a warm night off the bay!"

Down the line of the redoubt and near a small cluster of pines, he could see campfires where other watches were stationed. He shouldered his musket and strolled in the direction of the closest fire, which was the boundary of his own patrol. He had seen in the firelight that they had a drinking bucket, something he did not have, and his mouth was dry. A cool drink would help make the final hour on patrol more tolerable.

But as he drew nearer, he heard words that caused him to stop in his tracks, and move behind a twisted, needle-leafed scrub to listen without being seen.

"Dunmore is more a mercenary than the Germans," said one man on watch. It was Samuel, the man for whom Caleb had written pages of letters to send the man's wife when the war was done. "I heard he did bury them crates of silver on this island, 'cause with all he lost in Williamsburg, he is determined to get his wealth back in any way he can."

"Mmm," said another of the watch. Caleb knew this man only as Peter. He had never had reason to speak to him. "Mercenary, to be sure! And so am I. I wish I knew where that silver was hiding, I'd be at it with a shovel and out of here faster than a rooster after a hen. But Dunmore's got more than silver in mind for his fortune. There's the Ethiopian Regiment."

"What's that?" asked Samuel.

"Oh, haven't you heard? Word's all out and around, just out of the ears of the Negroes. Dunmore promised freedom to the escaped slaves and servants that joined him in Norfolk. Oh, and didn't he give 'em fancy uniforms and the like, something slaves would find to their liking, just like some Indians go for beads and other bright things."

"Yes," said Samuel, "but that regiment is good.

They fight hard. There's some men that look good when presenting themselves, and others that look good in a fight. The Ethiopians are both, Peter."

"I'm not doing anything but repeating what I've heard," said Peter. "But word is that when the war is over, Dunmore's sailing to the West Indies. He's gonna sell every last Negro down there, collect his pay, and go back to England for a well-needed rest with his family."

Caleb could no longer feel his feet beneath him on the sandy soil. His blood ran cold, and his fingers, wrapped about the butt of his musket, went numb.

"I should like some of that," continued Peter. "We've not been paid since the end of May. Anything to put a jingle in my haversack would be fair game to me. Give me a couple of them blacks and I'll take 'em to the West Indies myself!"

Caleb backed away as silently as he could, then moved along the southern trench to the edge of his line of watch. He paused, looking out across the black water that was the river, and knew in that moment what he had to do. Watch was over. His enlistment was over. He had to get Ammiel, Jospeh, and Galen, and they had to get out as soon as possible.

The men were snoring in their tents. Ammiel had had first watch. Joseph and Galen were scheduled for third watch. Caleb dropped beside Galen and shook him soundly.

"Wake up!" he whispered urgently. "Galen, wake up! We have to run!"

Galen flinched violently. His eyes flew open, and in the darkness, Caleb could read the terror in those eyes.

"What, Caleb?" he asked as he sat bolt upright.

"Where? Why?" He was already throwing on a shirt, and snatching in the darkness for his shoes. Instincts he had gained as a slave served him well. Instincts of action and survival.

"Ammiel, Joseph!" said Caleb, shaking the other two. "We have to run, now, or it may be too late! The sun is not up, so we should have cover of darkness. But we've got to get to the mainland, around the rebels, and find a place to hide!"

All three of Caleb's tent-mates were awake now, and pulling on clothing as quickly as they could. They seemed disoriented, but they were moving, trusting Caleb completely, even though he as of yet had not explained his early-morning alarm. As they laced up their shoes, Caleb said, "I've just heard that Dunmore has no plan whatsoever to give the Ethiopian Regiment their freedom when the war is done! I heard men talking, saying that the plan is to take up all to the West Indies and sell us into slavery!"

"No!" hissed Ammiel. "He wouldn't do that!"

"And why wouldn't he?" asked Caleb. "He lost nearly everything he had when he left his governorship, and would want to gain it back!"

"Sweet Jesus," said Joseph, raising one hand to heaven. "All in this world is deception, all this world is greed!"

And then, as if the devil had decided to answer instead of Sweet Jesus, there was a thunderous explosion outside the tent. Cannon fire. All four men clambered out, Ammiel still pulling into his shirt sleeves, and ran to the edge of the encampment. Other men had heard the noise, and were rolling from their tents, some naked, some in just linen shirts.

"Ships being fired on!" shouted Ammiel.

"The *Dunmore!*" came a scream from somewhere down the line of tents. "Rebels have shot a cannon at the *Dunmore!*"

Men raced for clothing, for weapons, and then ran for the western trenches along the river's side. Ethiopians, the 14th, the Queen's Own, all in various stages of dress and alertness, fell against the barricades and worked their muskets into place. Torches were lit and waved aloft by the youngest and most green of the units in order that the men could see what they were doing. Officers poured from tents, joining their regiments, shouting orders.

Caleb, Galen, Ammiel, and Joseph, all clutching their muskets and powder horns, slid into a trench beside Sergeant Freeman and a heavy contingency of their regiment. Freeman was already directing fire across the river, countering the shots the rebels were sending their way. Musket balls landed in sprays behind Caleb, striking trees, tents, and then, a man several yards away from Caleb. He had risen up to aim his newly loaded musket and the ball caught him in the throat. With a gush of blood and a silent gasp of disbelief, the man rolled his eyes in Caleb's direction, grabbed his neck, and fell backward.

Across the river, Caleb could see the flashing of the rebel rifles. He knew their weapons were fine hunting arms, and he knew their aim was better than that of the British with muskets. Then, to the right from up the river came a succession of bright, smoky cannon fire, several aimed at the ships on the river, several aimed at the island. There were shouts as cannon balls struck the sides of the barricades, and a scream as someone took a shot.

Caleb shouted to Galen, "We've got to get out!

What if we lose this battle and are taken captive by the rebels? What if we win, and Dunmore decides it is time to retire his vice admiralship and sail to the Southern Seas with the Ethiopians? Hold your musket! We have to make a dash!"

The smoke from the muskets was growing thick and pungent, and it became hard to see the river itself, much less the enemy on the other side. Some of the regiment halted their fire, waving their hands madly in front of their faces to clear their view. And then, though the waving had made little difference, began loading lead balls again and shooting over the water.

Sergeant Freeman shouted to his men to move to the west and closer to the shoreline to form a better and stronger defense against the heaviest of the rebel fire, and as the men, through the smoke and the deafening crack of rifle and musket fire, rose to obey this order, Caleb, Galen, Ammiel, and Joseph rose and moved quickly and quietly eastward along the trench. They crouched as they moved to avoid being struck and to avoid being seen.

They tripped over several men, dead and dying, on the sandy ground, but even with the cries for help from the wounded, Caleb forced himself onward. He knew where log canoes had been tied in a marshy inlet called Edwards Creek not far away. The canoes were used by the marines on scouting trips along the island's shores. These would be their only hope against the waters of the river. If they could get in and paddle southward and away from the heat of the battle, perhaps they could come ashore on the mainland where there was no fighting. And if there were a few snipers when they landed, they had their muskets, such as they were.

They reached the far end of the camp and climbed over the embankment with Caleb in the lead. Then they crossed several bridges that spanned island streams and moved into a grove of pines, staying in the thickest of the growth of trees. Caleb felt a dreadful responsibility hanging over him as he ran. These men were with him, live or die. Escape or be captured. This was nothing like the glorious daydream he'd had of the burning of the *Peggy Stewart.*

They reached Edwards Creek and slid down to the water's edge through brambles and scrub pines and reeds. Ammiel slipped and went under, then bobbed to the surface, still clutching his musket. "It's wet now," he laughed wildly, "but I don't think it's any worse for the wear! May even shoot better!"

There were three canoes with rough-hewn paddles, tied to low hanging branches of thorny locust trees. Caleb and Galen cut the knots of the ropes away with their bayonets, cutting their own hands on the spiked branches, and climbed into one canoe. Ammiel and Joseph followed suit into a second.

"We cross the river and hope for the best," said Caleb as he pushed from shore and the little canoe glided out into the river. "Watch and be ready to fire, but paddle and pray as well!"

Up the river the battle continued. The smoke was like a morning fog, relentless and acrid, hovering over the battalions and drifting down the river as if it did not want to let the four men be. From down the river, near the southeastern tip of the island, they could see ships heading their way from the bay. They had seen the smoke and had heard the cannons' roar, and they were moving swiftly to the aid of their fellow sailors.

"We have to get across now!" shouted Caleb. He braced his musket between his knees and dug the blade of the paddle into the water, forcing it across the river and against the current. He could hear Ammiel laughing in the other canoe; the man was either going mad or was reveling in the curious predicament in which he had found himself. Joseph grunted with each stroke of his paddle. Behind Caleb, Galen paddled in silence.

They reached the center of the river. Here, the current was stronger, and they drove the paddles in deeper and faster, fighting to keep from being spun around with the other floating debris. To their right the sun had begun to rise, cutting through the smoke-filled air with determined fingers of red and gold. The opposite shore was easier to see now. Caleb grit his teeth and leaned over the water with his paddle, thinking, *We can do this we are almost there yes yes yes we are almost there!* The canoe threatened to spin; Caleb and Galen forced it straight.

And then there was a flash from the shore, and the silhouette of a sniper in the trees, and Galen gasped and dropped his paddle. It whirled and tipped, then went the way of the leaves and sticks on the surface.

Immediately, Ammiel and Joseph aimed their loaded muskets at the sniper, and fired. They were nearly thrown out of the canoes with the impact, but braced themselves and straightened. The canoe veered to the left as the men reloaded.

Caleb reached back for Galen. His friend was clutching his arm, and the arm was bleeding profusely, but Galen hissed, "Paddle, Caleb! Get us out of this mess or I'll beat you senseless when we land and you know how well I can throw punches!"

Caleb drove his paddle back into the river water. Galen used the butt of his musket. In the second canoe, Ammiel and Joseph fired again, and the sniper in the trees dropped out of sight.

To the south came an explosion, and then a cannon ball was flying over their heads toward the thick of the battle. Caleb's teeth were clenched into his lower lip but they would not unlock. He tasted blood. He paddled harder. And the shore was just yards away.

Another cannon fired from the south. But it went well off course and struck the water just behind Caleb's canoe. The impact threw the tiny log boat over, hurling Caleb and Galen headlong into the water. Caleb plummeted to the river's depths, falling like a rock into the darkness. He could not tell up from down, and his hands battled the heavy growth of water weeds which wrapped his arms and torso. It seemed like an eternity that he struggled with the growth on the river bottom, and wondered if he would die here, victim of mindless river plants. His blood rushed in his ears. He gulped a mouthful of water and choked.

At last he opened his eyes to the brackish light and saw which way to swim. With strong kicks of his legs and strokes of his arms, he forced himself to the surface. His head broke through and he gasped, coughed, and gasped again.

Nearby he heard Ammiel and Joseph shouting. Through blurred eyesight he saw a paddle reaching out to him. He grasped it's slippery surface and did not let go.

"Don't let go, we're nearly there!" said Ammiel.

Caleb held the paddle as if it were the hand of God. He felt his body being pulled through the

water, and then his feet touched the bottom. He
lost it, then regained it. They had made it to shore.
Ammiel and Joseph's voices were blurry but urgent, first at a distance and then above him. Hands
took him beneath his shoulders and lifted him up.
His toes dragged the riverbank, and then he made
them take up their own burden. He planted his
feet and forced himself to walk. His musket was
gone as was his pouch of ammunition. But he
couldn't worry about that now.

The men moved through the trees as quickly as
they could. Caleb's vision cleared, and it was then
that he realized there were only three of them.

"Galen!" he said, turning around. "We can't
leave Galen!"

He began to move back to the river, but Ammiel
stopped him.

"He's gone, Caleb!"

"How do you know?" demanded Caleb. "Let me
go! I can swim! I can find him!"

"He's drowned!" insisted Ammiel. "We saw him
go, swept by the current, first his hands grabbing
for the surface and then disappearing. We
couldn't release you and go for him or both of
you would have been lost!"

God, oh God no! Caleb yanked free from Ammiel,
and stumbled toward the river. His heart slammed
against his ribs like cannon fire. His mind spun
like a log on the river. He reached the edge,
grasped the branch of a willow, and dropped to
his   knees
in the damp soil. His breaths came in painful
whoops. "You should have saved him!" he cried. "I
can swim, I would have made it! He needed help!"

"Caleb, he was too far away too quickly!"

"I should have saved him, then! I was his
friend!"

"You couldn't have, Caleb. He was gone in an instant."

Ammiel and Joseph stared at Caleb, and said nothing.

Not this! Father God please not this!

And Caleb bent over his own knees, and for the first time in years, he wept.

❧ 28 ❧

THEY HID A half-mile from the river the re-
mainder of the day, choking on the cannon
and musket smoke that found them in their hiding
place and listening for sounds of militia footfall.
Several times there was shouting and rustling, but
the rebels did not discover them where they lay,
huddled in a fern-covered crevice beneath a rotting log. By nighttime, the battle was spent.

Caleb, Ammiel, and Joseph had not spoken
since Galen had drowned in the river. All had
been alone with their thoughts, their decisions.
And so it did not come as a surprise to Caleb that
when they did speak they had different ideas of
what needed to be done.

"I ain't fighting nothing anymore," said Ammiel,
throwing his musket into the weeds by a stalwart
oak tree. In the twilight, he seemed much older
than his thirty years. Even his voice, which had
always been to Caleb an irritating yet lively nui-
sance, was slower, punctuated with grief and despair. "I'm gonna find my way west. There's land

far west of the colonies where nobody lives 'cept Indians. And Indians can't be much more savage than the rebels, or Lord Dunmore. Live alone, I will, and be free."

"Ammiel . . . ," began Caleb, but Ammiel held up his hand. His mind was made up. "Just pray God for my safe passage. There's many men between here and there who would have me for a slave again."

"I'll pray God for your safety," said Joseph.

Caleb nodded slowly. "As will I," he said.

"I'm returning to my master in Yorktown," said Joseph. "Heard tell the Virginians were offering humane and benevolent mercy to slaves who lay down arms and return humbly to their master's homes."

"But what is humane and benevolent to a master might not be humane and benevolent to a runaway," said Caleb.

"Perhaps not," said Joseph. But his mind was made up.

"And you, Caleb, horse handler from Maryland who has not a horse to handle?" asked Ammiel. "Where are you going?"

Caleb looked at the ground, then looked at the sky. Stars were out, dancing like fireflies, free and distant. "I don't know. I shall just go."

"North, south, or west?" asked Joseph.

Caleb shrugged. "My feet will tell me."

The three men bid each other farewell then. With quick embraces and wishes of fair providence, they went their separate ways. Ammiel took the forest to the west. Joseph walked the dense woods, heading south.

And after the others were long gone, Caleb's eyes drew his attention toward the north. And knew it was the way he needed to go.

❧ 29 ❧

December 10, 1776

Mr. Holt went to war last week, and has sent his wife and children to stay with her mother in Boston. The house and store are locked, with hopes the British will not come upon them and take them over for their own use.

I have worked for Mr. Jonathan Holt for these past three months, as part of his household in Philadelphia. I made safe passage from Virginia to Pennsylvania, after the battle on the island and escape from Dunmore, for my freeman paper was in my shirt, and though soaked from my plunge into the river, it was legible and thus acceptable, if not agreeable, to the men I met along the roadways.

Mr. Holt is a harness maker and the owner of a stable, and I was able to impress him with my ability at handling even the most grievously tempered animal. He hired me on, for board in his stable and a pound a month, for as a black I did not warrant a white man's pay. Yet he was a fair man, a Patriot, and not cruel and never a slave owner. He shared his newspapers

*with me when he learned I could read, and pen when
he learned I could write.*

*There was a declaration, adopted by the Continental
Congress in Philadelphia in July and published far
and wide not long afterward. I obtained a copy in
September. It reads in part:*

*"We hold these truths to be self-evident, that all men
are created equal, that they are endowed by their
Creator with certain unalienable Rights, that among
these are Life, Liberty, and the pursuit of Happiness."*

*And concluding, "For the support of this
Declaration, with a firm reliance on the protection of
divine Providence, we mutually pledge to each other
our Lives, our Fortunes, and our sacred Honor."*

*Benjamin Banneker told me that as a freeman I
have certain responsibilities. He also said that
sometimes one must be patient with the ills of the
present and to look ahead to a greater good. Life,
Fortune, and Sacred Honor. I own nothing, but I own
these three for I have myself. 'Tis something every man
should have.*

*I am going north to find the Continental Army. I
shall not be allowed to bear arms, but will do what I
can for this new and struggling country. The Congress
declared all men as equal. Perhaps their interpretation
of the word is narrow, and perhaps they do not mean
it to apply to slaves. But perhaps they will. If the
Patriots win, perhaps they will consider again at the
word equal.*

The word freedom.

🐝 30 🐝

PRIVATE BEN MARSHALL found his way to Caleb's campfire through the dark and the cold, and sat down on a snow-covered log. He didn't say anything for a long time, rubbing his rag-wrapped hands together and staring into the flame so intently Caleb thought the gaze might cause the flame to suddenly leap up into a bonfire with the sheer energy of the boy's concentration. Caleb waited silently. Nearby, soldiers in tattered blankets and ragged mitts stomped on the frozen ground, trying to keep their toes from freezing and snapping off. It was Christmas evening, 1776. Caleb turned seventeen that day. Christ was born yet again. Yet no one was singing carols. It took all the men had to stay alert and alive.

Ben clutched his knees with his fingers. Caleb could see the pale knuckles through the tangle of rags. The knuckles were cracked and tinged with blood. Caleb knew what the boy wanted, but it pained him to ask anything of the Negro who had no job but to gather wood, search for food, and care for the horses of Washington's spies when they came about.

Then the boy said, "Write a letter for me. I shall die over the river, I fear, and have nothing to give my mother for it other than my sad bones."

"I have no more paper or ink. If I did, it would be frozen, and my hands too cold to write."

Ben grimaced. Then he said, "I'll tell you, then. You remember it, you hear me? And write it when you have pen and paper to send her. She is Mrs. Jasper Simon in New York. You will remember?"

Caleb nodded. "I will."

The boy began to narrate, looking into the fire.

"Dear Mother," he said. His words puffed in the winter air. "It's cold here and snowy on the Pennsylvania banks of the Delaware. We've been seventeen days in this camp and it feels like seventeen years. The British and their German mercenaries are over the river, warm and fed, in the town of Trenton. I think they may be laughing at us over their Christmas pudding and ale. Why would they not? We have lost battle after battle. Long Island in August. New York in September. White Plains in October. We have been retreating for months. We hear that Cornwallis is returning to England soon to tell King George that we are defeated."

Not far from where Caleb and Ben sat on the frozen log was the rushing, ice-coated water of the Delaware River. Rumor among the men had been over the past three days that Washington was planning a move against the British on the other side. That very morning, Washington's sentries announced that they had taken every available boat to McKonkey's ferry, and had them drawn up there. Anticipation and anxiety spread like lice around the camp.

"Men have deserted," Ben continued. He picked at a rag on his hand as if it was a scab. Caleb remembered rags about the feet and hands of slaves. "Why would they not? The snow is relentless. We've no tents, some have no blankets, and others no shoes. Food is scarce, found by those with the energy to look and not always shared with those who cannot get up to look. Some of our men are waiting out their enlistment, which is over on January 1st. On that day, they will high it home. I do not blame them."

That afternoon, all the regiments were mustered near the General's tent, and after a brief Christmas service performed by the chaplain and a reading from Thomas Paine's essay "The American Crisis," General Washington himself came before the men. He walked their line with his hands behind his back, his cloak flapping wildly against the wind, his white, unpowdered hair covered with several turns of a scarf. He thanked the men for their courage and determination, then told them the plan. The British would never expect an attack on Christmas night, and in such weather. It was the hope that this would surprise them enough to give the Americans a victory. The soldiers eyed each other, some with uncertainty, others with expectation.

"But I could not leave, nor could I desert," said Private Ben Marshall. Caleb could see what looked like tears on the boy's cheeks, but it could have been only sleet that had pelted his face and melted there. "We only want what every man wants: freedom. We only demand what every soul demands: liberty! I shall stay with Washington and follow his lead, for a chain can break for one stressed link, and if there is a chance for liberty in this war, I will not be the cause of its defeat."

They would leave this camp and go to the boats any moment now, at the call of their commanders under Washington's direction. Caleb would act as a support, carrying supplies on his back, minding them on his boat and keeping them as dry as he could. He had no embroidered shirt, he had no Brown Bess nor bayonet. It was only because of his blanket, his pen and ink, his meager supply of food, and his knowledge of horses that had allowed Caleb to join with Washington's troops in mid-December.

But he knew he had come to the right place.

"Your loving son, Ben," said Ben.

Caleb smiled at the boy. "I will write it, and send it, but you should stay alive to sign it."

Ben got to his feet, shivered, and said, "I pray God you are right."

"But I ask payment," said Caleb.

"What? I have no pay! We've not seen wages in many weeks! You know that!"

"I ask one thing."

"What do you ask?"

"That you remember who wrote this letter for you. When the battle is done, win or lose, remember the man who carried your message for your mother."

"Your name is Caleb Jacobson," said Ben.

"Remember the man, Ben," said Caleb. "A man who wants what every man wants: freedom. Liberty. A man, Ben."

Ben frowned, then slowly his eyes softened. He nodded ever so slightly. "I will remember," he said.

Then he was gone in a swirl of new falling snow.

As the winter-white night rode its course, and

snow continued to pelt the weary, frozen men of the Continental Army beside the Delaware River, the call to muster came. The troops made way to the ferry where the boats awaited them on the river, and boarded to cross.

Caleb climbed into the back of a long Durham boat, minding the sacks of gunpowder and manning an oar. The trees across the wide waterway seemed to wave to the men with gray, skeletal arms. Caleb could not know what they knew, what premonition they held, what greeting, or what warning. He could not know if the battle into which the Patriots were going was ordained to be a victory or a dreadful loss. If a win, liberty from King George would still be possible. If a loss, there would be no more chances.

"Galen," he said softly as the tip of his oar cut through a sheet of thin ice, "I do this for you. For Fern. I do this for Ammiel and Joseph and Benjamin Banneker. I do it for the slave and for the freeman. I even do this for Mr. Whitley, so men such as he may have the chance someday to see the error in their thought, and be brought closer to God for the understanding."

"What is that you said?" asked a bloody-footed soldier next to him with his oar.

Caleb answered, "It was just a prayer, my friend."

"For victory?"

"Indeed. Oh, indeed."